:: Leaving Simplicity

:: Leaving Simplicity

BY CLAIRE CARMICHAEL

annick press
toronto + new york + vancouver

ANNICK PRESS LTD.

First published by Random House Australia Pty Limited, Sydney, Australia, 2006.
This edition published by arrangement with Random House Australia.

Copyedited and proofread by *Elizabeth McLean*
Cover illustration: (cityscape) © *istockphoto.com/Juergen Sack;* (circuit board)
© *istockphoto.com/Steven Foley;* (shopping cart) © *istockphoto.com/Eva Serrabassa;*
(hand) © *istockphoto.com/Edward McIntyre*
Cover design: *Sheryl Shapiro*
Interior design: *Diane Yee, Electra Design Group*
Creative direction: *Lisa Eng-Lodge, Electra Design Group*

CATALOGUING IN PUBLICATION

Carmichael, Claire
    Leaving simplicity / Claire Carmichael.
Previously published under title: Ads r us.

ISBN 978-1-55451-090-0 (bound)
ISBN 978-1-55451-089-4 (pbk.)

    I. Title.

PR6053.A6853L43 2007   j823'.914   C2007-902534-X

PRINTED AND BOUND IN CANADA

Annick Press is committed to protecting our natural environment. As part of our efforts, this book is printed on Enviro paper: it contains 30% post-consumer recycled fibers, is acid-free, and is processed chlorine-free.

Published in the U.S.A. by
Annick Press (U.S.) Ltd.

Distributed in Canada by
Firefly Books Ltd.
66 Leek Crescent
Richmond Hill, ON
L4B 1H1

Distributed in the U.S.A. by
Firefly Books (U.S.) Inc.
P.O. Box 1338
Ellicott Station
Buffalo, NY 14205

Visit our website at **www.annickpress.com**

FOR SHEILA

:: Prologue

"Uncle Paul, it's too dangerous," Barrett said. As if to prove the point, lightning sizzled through the charged air. A deafening thunderclap followed almost immediately.

The man's red beard bristled as he glared a challenge at the sky. "I'm not afraid of Nature's fireworks."

Earlier, when the harvesters had gone inside for lunch, the wheat field had been bathed in sunshine, although purple-black clouds had been massing behind the hills. Now those clouds boiled with menace directly overhead, hungry tongues of lightning flickering.

Renquist's thin face was creased with worry. "Leader Paul, Barrett's right. It is too dangerous to go out into the open. Wait here until the storm passes."

Several others in the group murmured agreement. "Remember the cattle killed by a lightning strike last year," someone said.

The red-bearded man shook himself free from Renquist's detaining hand. "It's a dry storm, moving quickly. By the time I've started the tractor, it will have passed."

He stomped off in the direction of the farm machinery in the middle of the paddock.

"Uncle Paul!" the boy called, but his voice was drowned by a mighty crack of thunder.

Renquist said, "Barrett, you stay here. All of us will wait until it's safe."

Wind howled through the trees sheltering the compound. A few fat drops of rain splattered onto the dusty ground. Ignoring this, the stout figure plodded towards the tractor.

The blinding flash and deafening crack were simultaneous. Ears were set ringing. A strange metallic smell filled the air. When, blinking, they could see again, the man had disappeared.

With a hiss, the rain began.

They found him spread-eagled in the wheat. Grunting with his dead weight, they carried the body back through the pelting rain. There was a scorch mark down one side of his face and his ginger whiskers were seared, but otherwise he looked as if in peaceful sleep.

As second-in-command, Renquist now automatically became Leader Renquist. After the bell had tolled to signify a death in the community, Leader Renquist directed that the body be washed, dressed in white overalls, and placed in a plain wooden coffin. This would lie open in the church for at least a day to allow mourners to pay their respects to the man who had founded the community and led them for so many years.

Once the body was placed in the front of the church, Renquist took the boy aside. "I must contact your uncle's sister. I believe she's your only living relative. Decisions have to be made about your future."

"Decisions? I'll stay here at Simplicity, won't I?"

"That's for your aunt to say."

"But I've never even met her."

Renquist patted his shoulder consolingly. "It's likely she'll have no interest in moving you to the city."

The fatal lightning strike occurred on a Thursday. On Saturday Barrett's aunt, Kara Trent, came to Simplicity.

1 :: Taylor

"Fifty meters to your left is the intersection you require," prompted the Nav system. Its artificial voice remained cheerful as it added, "Extreme caution is advised. This is a designated Code Thirteen Rural Route."

"Thirteen?" I said. "I've never been on anything worse than Code Three."

"Then it will be a new experience for you," said my mother dryly, as she turned off the highway onto a narrow dirt track.

Although we were in Mom's latest luxury sedan, the vibration from the rutted dirt surface was still enough to loosen teeth. Twisting around, I could see clouds of brown dust billowing behind us. We were in the middle of absolutely nowhere, surrounded by boring bush. The only sign of life was a black crow flapping overhead. Complete drekdom.

"Remind me again why I'm here, Mom."

"Don't start, Taylor."

Typical. My mother's a total tyrant who always gets her own way. I dug around in my bag and grabbed my Om. I'd call Gabi and send her a photo of this unbelievable dirt road we were bouncing along.

My mother glanced over at me, frowning. "Put that away. You can last five minutes without communicating with your friends. Besides, we're almost there."

I shoved my Om back in my bag and glared at the Nav's screen on the dashboard. She was right. The display showed our car as a moving red dot almost at the end of a winding road that petered out into blank nothingness. Actually there *was* something there; that'd be Simplicity Center, this strange ecological place that my uncle started a zillion years ago. I'd never visited Simplicity, and had no interest in it whatsoever, but this morning my mother had insisted I keep her company.

Along the bottom of the Nav screen an advertisement scrolled for the latest voice-activated Resonic Earbud. No one I knew had one yet, and I wanted to be the first.

"For my birthday, can I have a Resonic Earbud? *Please*, Mom? It's what I really, really want. It's so cool! Like, it's a little capsule you shove deep in your ear. You can call your friends, listen to the latest music, get the star goss—"

"I'm well aware of the marketing campaign for the Resonic Earbud. The answer's no."

"Oh, *Mom!*"

"How many communication devices have you got now,

Taylor? You don't use all of them, so you hardly need another one."

When she had that cold tone in her voice, she really meant it. I'd have to get to work on my dad. At least *he* wanted me to be happy.

A few more dumb trees swished by. "This is boooring." No reply. "I still don't see why you had to drag me along," I said, knowing the whine in my voice was practically guaranteed to put Mom's teeth on edge. "You know I wanted to go with Gabi this afternoon to the auditions for *Ugly-D to Teen Queen*."

Mom clicked her tongue impatiently. "Neither you nor Gabi by any stretch of the imagination can be described as an ugly duckling in need of a makeover."

"Gabi's always saying her nose is too big. She'd jump at a chance to have a new one for nothing."

My mother glanced over at me with a thin smile. "And what about you? Is there something else you'd like to change about yourself?"

I had to think about that. My parents had already sprung for plastic surgery to reshape my chin. "I'd like longer legs," I said.

"We've discussed this before. You're not getting extension implants."

Folding my arms, I sank down as low as I could in the seat. "Being a contestant on *Ugly-D* would be so great. You get a complete makeover from head to toe, and *everybody* watches the show, so you end up famous. And the winner, the Teen Queen, gets to star in a movie, guaranteed."

My mother acted like she hadn't heard a word I'd said. "Taylor, I'm expecting you to behave appropriately when we arrive at Simplicity Center."

"Yeah, yeah."

My mother shot me one of her laser looks. "We're here to pay our respects to my brother, your uncle. And don't bother to say you've never met him—I know that. The point is your cousin has no one but us. We're Barrett's only living relatives."

As if I cared. "Barrett?" I said. "Dumb name."

That got me another freezing glance. "He's just lost the person who's brought him up since he was a baby. I imagine he's grieving."

"Boo hoo."

"*Taylor...*"

I was suddenly embarrassed with myself. I couldn't even begin to imagine what it must be like to lose someone really close.

"All right," I said, "I'll be nice." An awful thought struck me. "You're not going to tell me we're taking him home with us, are you?"

"It's possible."

"Mom, you've got to be joking! Like, he's a farmie. Can you see him fitting in?"

"Not another word, Taylor. It's got nothing to do with you."

"If he's going to live in our house, it's got *everything* to do with me."

"The subject's closed."

Typical! I turned my head away and stared out the window. The bush had given way to paddocks, fenced with barbed wire. I saw a herd of black and white cows, then we turned a corner and the road ended. A high, barred gate faced us. On it was a large sign. Black letters on a stark white background read:

SIMPLICITY CENTER
TRESPASSERS WILL BE FORCIBLY REMOVED

"This is going to be fun, fun, fun," I said, half under my breath. Mom ignored me.

After a few horn blasts, an old guy turned up, wearing droopy overalls and a straw hat. "Yes?" he said in a raspy voice after Mom had put down her window.

"I'm Paul Trent's sister, Kara." When he shifted his glance to me, Mom added in an irritated voice, "And this is Taylor, Paul's niece."

"You're expected." Without another word, he opened the gate, giving us a blank stare as we rumbled over a metal grid.

I got out my Om and took a shot of him. Gabi would never believe this place. I looked back to see him closing the gate behind us. "Friendly type."

Mom didn't answer, being fully taken with guiding our car over a heavily rutted track even worse than the road we'd just been traveling on. A few bone-rattling minutes later we stopped outside what seemed to be the main building. A large single-story place painted mud brown, it had narrow windows and a red, corrugated iron roof. Near the front door a big brass bell was hanging in a heavy wooden frame. Other, smaller buildings, all painted the same horrible brown, and with the same red roofs, were clustered around. The one exception was a small, white building, standing off by itself.

As we got out of the air-conditioned car, a blast of heat hit us. A short, square woman came rushing up, her starched apron glaringly white in the bright sunshine. Her hair was cut short, and it was *gray*. When was the last time I'd seen anyone with gray hair?

"Welcome to Simplicity! I'm Jane-Marie."

"Kara Trent. And this is my daughter, Taylor."

She actually shook hands with us, like they used to do in olden times, before the Plagues. When she wasn't looking, I wiped my fingers with a tissue.

It was obvious the woman was impressed by my mother. Most people are. Mom's tall and thin, with masses of auburn hair and wide blue eyes. And she spends a lot of money on clothes. Today she was wearing practically skin-tight red leather pants and jacket, and black high-heeled boots.

Jane-Marie continued to smile as she said, "The moment I saw your vehicle, I sent a message to Barrett. He'll be here any moment."

Her smile vanished as she pointed in the direction of the white building. "But first, perhaps you'd like to visit the chapel. You'll be desiring to spend a few private moments with your brother. He's in an open coffin."

My mother did a total double-take. "An open coffin? Paul was struck by lightning, wasn't he?"

"When Leader Paul's soul was released, there was very little damage to his physical shell."

"Oh, yeetch!" I said. "Don't ask me to look at a dead body."

Jane-Marie stared at me as though I'd said something weird. Then, obviously relieved, she said, "Here's Barrett."

My cousin wouldn't have been bad-looking, if he'd had a decent haircut and been wearing proper clothes, not a faded pair of khaki overalls and an old denim shirt. He was tall and had broad shoulders. His hair was a darker red than Mom's and he had the same blue eyes. There were freckles sprinkled across his nose and cheeks. Disgusting! No one I knew had them—you got them zapped as soon as they appeared.

"Here is your aunt, Kara Trent," Jane-Marie said to him. "And her daughter, your cousin, Taylor."

Just like she had, he put out his hand. My mother shook with him, but I put mine behind my back.

"You spread germs that way," I said. "Haven't you heard of the Plagues?"

Grinning, he dropped his hand. Not bad teeth for

someone who had probably never even seen a dentist. "You won't catch anything from me," he said, "but since you come from the outside world, perhaps I should be worried about touching *you*, Cousin Taylor."

Cousin Taylor? What a bleeb!

2 :: Barrett

My name is Barrett Trent. I became an orphan when I was almost eight months old. I'd been in the back seat in a baby restraint when my parents' car collided head-on with a truck that had veered onto the wrong side of the mountain road. My mother and father died instantly. So did the truck driver. I was unhurt.

It's impossible, I suppose, but sometimes I think I can remember the glaring headlights, the screech of brakes, the rending crash, and then silence, broken by my thin cry.

I'd been left in the world with only two close relatives—my father's brother and sister, Paul and Kara. Uncle Paul was the one to take me in and bring me up. My Aunt Kara I had never met. Until today.

She'd arrived in a long black vehicle that looked totally out of place at Simplicity, where all we had was farm machinery and battered pickup trucks. Under the layer of dust, words glowed in luminescent red, moving continuously around Aunt Kara's car like an endless ribbon unrolling:

ADS-4-LIFE COUNCIL...IMPROVING
YOUR WORLD EVERY DAY...

The name was familiar to me. My uncle had spent many hours warning me about the role of advertising in the Chattering World. He'd been particularly scathing about the influential lobbying organization his sister headed, the Ads-4-Life Council.

When I met my aunt and cousin, I tried to be courteous, and not stare. They both wore jewelry, which was discouraged at Simplicity, and I'd never seen embarrassingly tight outfits like the ones they were wearing. My Aunt Kara looked a bit like me, only thinner. My cousin, Taylor, was skinny too. She'd missed the red hair in the family. Hers was brown with lighter streaks, and she wore it in an odd system of plaited strands with purple ribbon threaded through it.

Aunt Kara looked around, her hands on her hips. From her expression, she didn't find the view pleasing. "I suppose I'd better see my brother. I understand there's to be a service of some sort."

"We were waiting for your arrival," said Jane-Marie. "The funeral ceremony is scheduled for two o'clock this afternoon. I hope that suits you?" She waited until Aunt Kara nodded assent, then gestured towards our chapel. "Would you come this way?"

"Don't trouble yourself. Barrett can take us."

"Oh, of course." Jane-Marie's shoulders slumped. I

knew she dearly loved to be involved in anything interesting, and on an interest scale of one to ten, my aunt and
cousin rated at least eleven. Not only did they come from
the forbidden outside world in a luxurious vehicle, the
like of which we'd never seen here before, they were also
wearing bright colors. Aunt Kara dazzled in eye-popping
red and my cousin in a deep purple tunic. No one at
Simplicity ever wore anything so intense. Our clothes
were all in muted shades.

"Please accompany us," I said. Cousin Taylor wrinkled
her nose and muttered something under her breath,
apparently not impressed by Jane-Marie, which was a pity,
because she was one of the kindest people I knew.

"I'll stay in the car," my cousin announced.

"You'll come with us," Aunt Kara said. From her tone, it
seemed she was used to being obeyed instantly.

Taylor mumbled something, then, pouting, dawdled
along behind as we set off towards the chapel.

There was no one inside... well, no one alive. Uncle Paul
lay in his plain wooden coffin. Even from the doorway I
could see the great beak of his nose jutting into the air.
Jane-Marie slid into a pew at the back and sank to her
knees to pray.

Aunt Kara didn't hesitate, but marched up and stood
staring down at her brother. Taylor waited at the doorway,
looking rather sick.

I felt sorry for her. It was a shock the first time you
saw someone from whom the life had fled. Myself, I'd

seen several dead bodies, and assisted in preparations for burial. Just a few hours earlier I'd washed Uncle Paul, dressed him in his best overalls, combed his beard and hair, and with the help of Leader Renquist, lifted him into his coffin.

"Cousin, are you all right?" I asked.

"I'm fine." She was half a head below my height, and she glared up at me as though I'd done something wrong. I liked her dark gray eyes. Folding her arms, she leaned against the side of the doorway. "I'll stay here."

After a moment I walked up the aisle and joined my aunt. I slid my eyes sideways, wondering if she'd cry. It didn't seem likely.

"Surely Paul should have been dressed in a suit," she said, frowning at the overalls on my uncle's body.

"We don't have formal clothing at Simplicity."

She gave an irritated sigh. "And what in the hell was Paul doing out in the middle of a thunderstorm? My brother always was pigheaded. I suppose someone warned him not to go out, so he did." This was so close to the truth, I almost smiled.

She gave me an appraising look. "Well, Barrett, I can say this—you don't seem very upset."

"I'm sorry Uncle Paul is dead."

Inwardly, I was guilty I didn't feel more. What I did feel was a sort of emptiness, I suppose because Uncle Paul had had so much influence on my life. Of course I regretted that he'd been killed, but he'd been a cold man who had never permitted argument or discussion about his views, being convinced he was always right. And he had rarely missed an opportunity to tell me how lucky I was that he'd taken me in, a helpless infant who, without his intervention, likely would have gone to a foster home in the Chattering World.

"You would have ended up with strangers," Uncle Paul often said. "Your Aunt Kara wouldn't have taken you. She's not inclined to be charitable, at least, not unless there's something in it for her."

My aunt gave a last glance at Uncle Paul's face, and turned to leave. "I suppose I can hardly fail to attend my brother's funeral. In the meantime, you can show me around Simplicity Center."

I wanted to ask her what she intended to do about me, but had no opportunity to bring up the subject, as she set off for the main building at a rapid pace, firing questions at Jane-Marie as she strode along. Taylor and I followed behind the two contrasting figures—one short and comfortably plump, the other tall and thin.

When they reached the front door, Aunt Kara swept through it, ignoring the curious glances of a couple of children who were lingering beside the assembly bell. Edward and Chrissie had obviously sneaked out of the library to see the extraordinary strangers who'd arrived from the outside world.

Jane-Marie murmured a few words to the two truants. Whatever she said sent them scuttling back to their books without even trying to argue. Then she went off to supervise final preparations for my uncle's wake.

I followed my aunt and cousin inside. Aunt Kara was stalking around, checking out the rooms. Taylor drifted along behind her mother, looking as if she wished she were anywhere but here. I followed them, wincing. The heels of Aunt Kara's high-heeled boots beat a hard tattoo on the polished wooden floors, and she slammed doors and opened cupboards without a thought for the noise she was making. At Simplicity we were taught the importance of quietness and harmony. Clearly these were not qualities my aunt held dear.

She marched down a hallway, heading for the door at the end. I hurried to catch up with her. "Aunt Kara, please don't go in there. It's a stillness space and—"

She flung open the door, had a quick look around, then said to me, "What are they doing? Praying?"

There were eight people sitting on the floor of the bare room, each with legs crossed, eyes closed and hands relaxed on their knees. No one acknowledged the interruption, but of course they could hear my aunt's penetrating voice.

"Meditating," I said in a whisper, "about Uncle Paul's life."

Behind me, Taylor muttered, "Freakoids."

I turned around. "What's a freakoid?"

Her lip curled. "You wouldn't want to know."

Aunt Kara stepped back into the hallway and shut

the door firmly. "I gather this Simplicity cult my brother started doesn't use any of the electronic devices of the modern world. Yes?"

"That's correct."

She peered at me. "Have you ever seen a television program?"

I shook my head. Taylor snickered.

"Never?"

"Never."

She seemed pleased. "How about radio?"

"No."

"Recorded music? Mobile phones? Interactive games?"

"Nothing like that, although in theory I understand how most of them operate."

"You do? How did that come about?"

"Uncle Paul said to defeat evil you must know its ways."

Hands on hips, my aunt threw back her head and laughed. "Evil? How typical of my brother. He always was paranoid about mind control. Ironic, really, since that's what he's done to *you*. He's manipulated what you think and feel by depriving you of all the comforts of modern life."

"You poor thing," said Taylor, rolling her eyes.

They didn't understand. I felt the need to explain what Simplicity stood for. "Uncle Paul developed the philosophy of the uncomplicated existence. Plain living in tune with nature. Simplicity in all things. He believed the world outside not only destroyed the ecosystem, but it also destroyed one's peace of mind, one's essential core."

I could almost hear my uncle's deep, soft voice repeating the words as I said them. It was odd to think he was gone forever, and I'd never again experience the weight of his overbearing personality.

Aunt Kara tilted her head, looking at me with narrowed eyes. "Do you always talk this way?"

"I beg your pardon?"

"Like you're reading out of some old book?"

I raised my shoulders. "It was the way I was taught."

She gave me a cool, almost calculating look. "Do you know what advertisements are?"

"Public announcements designed to sell something to as many people as possible."

"Have you ever seen a print ad? In a magazine perhaps? Or newspaper?"

"We don't have newspapers or magazines at Simplicity."

She leaned closer to me, so I could smell her perfume. It had a musky scent I didn't particularly like. "Barrett, you're telling me you've never, ever seen an ad?"

"We barter eggs or grain for items we can't make ourselves, so sometimes I've seen what you might call advertisements on the side of trucks when someone from the outside has come to trade."

"Apart from that, you've never seen an ad. Is that correct?"

She was sounding like my uncle when he was badgering me over something. He'd go on and on until it was easier to give in than to argue. "I know what advertisements are," I said. "Uncle Paul explained how they use the techniques of persuasion."

Aunt Kara nodded, satisfied. "It's clear you're an ad virgin. Now, how about computers, handheld or otherwise?"

"I've never seen one."

"Unbelievable!" said Taylor, rolling her eyes again.

My aunt beamed at me. "I believe I'll find your reactions to the modern world very, very interesting, Barrett."

"Mom! You're *not!* You *can't...*"

Ignoring her, Aunt Kara said to me, "When your parents died, leaving a helpless baby alone in the world, Paul and I discussed whether I should be the one to bring you up."

"Why didn't you?" I asked, sincerely interested.

She shrugged gracefully. "At the time all my energy was going into establishing my career. And Paul was very keen to raise you in what he called an untainted ecosystem."

"You make me sound like a package to be passed around."

My aunt raised one eyebrow. It was clear she didn't expect to be criticized, however mildly. "I'm making up for it now. How long will it take you to pack your things?"

My stomach clenched. "I was hoping to stay here at Simplicity, Aunt Kara."

"I'm afraid that's impossible. You're coming home with us."

"But—"

"Don't bother arguing," Taylor said. "You'll find my mother always gets her own way. Give in. It's easier." She hunched her shoulders and turned her back to us. I heard her mumble, "You'll be sorry," but whether this was directed at her mother or me wasn't clear. Perhaps it was to both of us.

Aunt Kara checked her watch, which was impossibly delicate and both the casing and the band appeared to be made of gold. "You'll have time to get your things together before the service. I'll speak with the new head of your cult. Renquist's his name, isn't it?"

"Yes, Leader Renquist. I'm sure he wouldn't mind me staying—"

"Not an option, Barrett. I'll explain to Renquist you're leaving to be with your family. While I'm doing that, pack only what's absolutely necessary." She looked me over. "You won't need much. Any clothes like the ones you're wearing, for example, are totally unsuitable." Her glance went to my feet. Grimacing, she added, "And the boots most definitely can be left behind."

Feeling a sting of resentment at her disparaging words, I said, "I only have boots. Unless you want me barefoot...?"

My tone, I knew, was close to disrespectful. Cousin Taylor shot me a surprised look. Aunt Kara gave a small, tight smile. "So you have some spirit. I'm pleased to see it. Now, please give me directions to find Renquist, then go and pack your things. We'll leave directly after my brother's funeral."

Although the sun was still shining outside, the day seemed suddenly gray and depressing. How could I say goodbye to everyone at Simplicity? And what about Jessica?

"My friends—" I began.

"You'll make new friends," my aunt said briskly. "Change is good. It leads to personal growth. You're used to a situation where everything is static, inflexible. The world you're about to join is so much more exciting and challenging."

"Aunt Kara, truthfully, I'd rather stay at Simplicity."

"I'm sorry," she said. There was no sympathy in her voice or on her face. "It's understandable you want to cling to the familiar, but you're in no position to judge what's best for you. I am."

I felt as though a huge weight was crushing me down. It was obviously fruitless to continue protesting. My aunt was implacable. She would never change her mind.

3 :: Taylor

Since I'd never even met my mother's brother, I didn't see why I had to go to his funeral, but Mom insisted like I knew she would, saying we had to pay proper respect to my uncle's memory, even if we didn't agree with anything he stood for. A place had been saved for us with Barrett in the very front pew of the chapel, really close to the open coffin. I didn't want to, but I couldn't help sneaking a look at the dead face. Yetch!

The Simplicity people crowded into the pews behind us. I turned around to look them over. Everyone wore peculiar, old-fashioned work clothes, as if they were in some ancient farming movie.

"Eyes front," hissed my mother.

Oh, right! Eyes front meant I had to confront my uncle's dead body. His skin seemed sort of waxy, as if he wasn't real, and his bushy red beard looked like it was glued on. I imagined what would happen if he suddenly took a breath and sat up. Probably people would scream and faint. Not my mother, though. She'd probably order him to lie down again, so we could get on with his funeral.

I glanced over at Barrett, who was sitting on my mother's other side. He was so pale his freckles stood out, and he was biting his lip. At least one person was sorry Uncle Paul was dead.

When the creaky old organ started up, sounding like it had a bad case of asthma, everyone stood and began singing. Mom handed me a hymnbook, but no way was I going to make a fool of myself over something I'd never heard before. She sang, though, and so did Barrett. And there was someone behind us belting out the words in the loudest, off-key voice. I sneaked a look and found it was the fat little woman who'd greeted us when we'd arrived.

The hymn went on, verse after verse, then the Leader Renquist guy went on forever about Uncle Paul's life and achievements. Achievements? I couldn't see there were many of those, as my uncle had spent most of his time setting up this Simplicity place and running it like some bizarre private community.

Some lady who looked about a thousand years old got up and rambled on about the environment and how Uncle Paul had proved it was possible to live in complete harmony with nature. Another hymn, all about harvests and plenty, followed. Then different people came up to the front and said more things about Uncle Paul.

I don't know why, but it started me thinking what would be said about *me* at *my* funeral. It made me feel quite sad, and I actually got tears in my eyes, but nobody noticed, luckily. I wouldn't have wanted anyone to think I was sobbing over someone I didn't even know.

Barrett was the last to speak. He didn't cry, but his voice was a bit shaky. He thanked Uncle Paul for giving him a home and for instructing him about the world and all that was in it. Beside me, Mom gave a contemptuous snort. It was clear she didn't think much of anything my uncle had done as far as teaching Barrett was concerned. Surprise! For once, I agreed with her over something.

The next bit was really foul. Two guys with hammers came forward to fit the top on the coffin and nail it down, right there in front of us all. I couldn't watch. What if he was still alive, and being sealed into the box forever? He'd wake up when it was too late, and scream and pound on the top, but no one would hear him. Too dire!

"Taylor!" snapped my mother. I realized everyone else was standing. They watched silently as four men carried the closed coffin out of the chapel, followed by Barrett. Then we all trooped after them until we reached an open grave that, judging by the piles of fresh dirt nearby, had just been dug.

Ropes were used to lower the coffin into the hole. Once it was in position, there were more prayers about how we all were part of the great cycle of life and death. Mega morbid! Everyone had eyes shut and head bowed— I looked, so I knew even Mom had closed her eyes. After the last amen, there was the horrible hollow sound of clods of dirt being shoveled onto the top of the coffin.

Mom was as impatient to get away as I was, but we had to go to Uncle Paul's wake, which was held in a nearby assembly hall. There were tables loaded with food. Of course it had to be all home-cooked—I doubt these people ever even went near a supermarket. And I couldn't believe it—I was handed a real plate to use, not a throwaway one. Without a dishwasher, cleaning up after this would be dire!

I tried a mouthful of one stew thing, which I didn't much like. After that I stuck to crusty bread, which was actually not too bad with soft, yellow butter.

::

At last Mom announced we were getting out of there. Everyone bunched around Barrett to say goodbye. One girl—I heard him call her Jessica—sort of clutched his arm and cried. Nobody else looked much happier. Barrett seemed a bit sick about the whole thing. His face was white and his lips were pressed tightly together. I guess I'd feel that way too, if I'd spent my whole life here and didn't know anything better.

When we finally made it to the car, Barrett put his bag, a beaten-up old canvas thing, in the trunk. "Is that all you're taking?" I said.

"I haven't got much."

Mom said Barrett should sit in the front seat, as he'd never been outside Simplicity before, and had lots to see. I didn't mind because it would give me a chance to make myself comfortable in the back and call Gabi or watch a movie or listen to music.

The Simplicity people crowded around the car looking as miserable as Barrett did. At last Mom managed to pull away, with everyone waving and calling out. When we were through the gate and back on the rough dirt road, Barrett blew his nose hard. And he used a handkerchief! I leaned over from the back seat to check it out. Only old, old ladies used handkerchiefs anymore.

"Don't you have tissues?" When he gave me a blank look, I said, "You know—paper hankies—you blow your nose on them and then throw them away."

He shook his head. "Tissues are a wasteful use of wood pulp. At Simplicity we only use handkerchiefs."

This guy was a real drupe.

He didn't say anything more, but hunched his shoulders and stared out the front of the car. If I was going to rely on Barrett for entertaining conversation, it was going to be a looong wait. I couldn't watch a movie, because the ruts in the road made the car vibrate so much it was impossible. We rattled along the track for ages, then finally hit the smooth surface of the decent road.

I didn't bother with a movie, but hit the satellite station button for my customized play list. Mom hadn't let me put my music on while we'd been on our way to Simplicity, but I figured she'd be more relaxed now that we were returning to civilization. Sound filled the car. Cool! It was Fried Eyes' latest.

"Turn that cacophony off!" commanded my mother, as Barrett put his hands over his ears.

Jeez! I punched the button. "Well, excuse me! All I wanted was a little music."

"That was *music?*" asked Barrett, putting his hands down.

Mom gave a snort of laughter. "That's what my daughter and her friends call it. I don't." She gave my cousin a curious glance. "Apart from the chapel, you don't have music at Simplicity?"

"There's a piano. We have sing-alongs and people with good voices do solos. Nothing as loud as this."

"If you think *that's* loud," I said, "you're in for quite a few surprises."

I gave up on watching a movie or playing a sim game and I decided not to call Gabi or Delia, because watching my cousin turned out to be a lot of fun. He kept twisting around, looking at everything like he'd just dropped in from another planet—which I suppose in a way he had.

He really stared at the moving pictures on the first billboard we came to, and he jumped when voices and music suddenly boomed at us, selling Magnotoonie Brain Tuners. *Fine tune your neural pathways! Use Magnotoonie Brain Tuners for optimum mental clout!*

Something was puzzling him. He frowned as he looked back over his shoulder at the billboard. "Why's it still so loud? Shouldn't it get softer as we get farther away?"

"Directional audio," said my mother. "Imagine a funnel

of sound focused like a searchlight. It picks up our vehicle and remains fixed on us, until we're out of range."

Before we reached the next billboard, she punched a code into the keypad beside the steering wheel. When we passed the next one in total silence, Barrett said, "Is that billboard malfunctioning?"

"It won't switch on for us. I've activated an override, so that any we pass from now on won't respond."

"Does everyone get this override? Or do they just have to put up with all that noise?"

I had to laugh. Only a very few select people could turn advertising off. And Mom's response was her predictable rant about the importance of ads. "Advertising is a vital component of our culture, Barrett. It would never do to have override technology widely available, as it's essential that everyone be exposed to information on products and services. Advertising is an indispensable element in our way of life. It educates the public, and pays for so many things we take for granted."

"Are they all things we really need?"

Mom looked at Barrett sharply, like he was having a joke at her expense, but when she saw he was serious, she said, "You'll find you have to be open to many new ideas about how the real world functions."

"Real world? I grew up in a real world." With a faint smile, he added, "Uncle Paul called everywhere outside Simplicity the Chattering World. He said it was full of noise and confusion."

"My brother had some very unconventional ideas, Barrett. It's a pity he didn't allow you to be exposed to civilization. As it is, you're at a distinct disadvantage. There's so much you need to know to effectively function in society. The history of advertising, for example, is one of the compulsory courses in your data paradigm."

Oh, *groan!* Lecture five thousand and six. Luckily, before Mom could really get going, Lloyd came through on a satjump. Soon she was giving a stream of instructions to her assistant.

"Say hi from me," I said. Lloyd was sooo sexy. He had these deep blue eyes and the greatest smile.

Mom didn't bother to pass on my hi, but continued with all the things she wanted Lloyd to do. He had to be ready to leap to attention any time, day or night, which was pretty much the same for everyone around my mother, including me. My country cousin had *no* idea what living in our home was going to be like, poor bleeb.

Right now, he was looking confused at the voice coming out of nowhere, so I took pity on him.

"It's a satjump." He looked even more confused. "A satellite jump. The car's linked to a satellite that knows exactly where we are all the time. Lloyd's call jumped up to the satellite, and the satellite directed it down to the car."

"Like a mobile telephone?"

"You know what a mobile is?"

"Of course."

I was guessing he didn't have a clue. "So you've used one, have you?"

"No. But I understand how they work."

Oh, sure he did! Honestly, this guy was unbelievable. "What if there's some big disaster at Simplicity," I said, "and you have to get help from outside? What do you do? Send smoke signals?"

"We offer agistment to the farmer who owns the adjacent property. In return we have the use of Mr. Carter's telephone for emergencies."

"What's agistment?"

"We let some of his livestock pasture on our land. That's agistment."

Like, this was gripping stuff. "Fascinating," I said.

Barrett went back to staring out the window. I noticed him wincing every time we zoomed past huge semi-trailers. "I've never seen so many vehicles together at one time," he said. "Or going so fast."

"But you can drive?"

"Farm machinery—tractors, trucks."

"That's a lot of help."

Barrett twisted around to look at me. "I'm sure you understand I'm finding everything rather strange."

He sounded a bit put out, as if I should be more sympathetic. But I hadn't wanted him to come home with us—it was all Mom's idea. I mean, I wouldn't make things difficult for Barrett, but basically, it was nothing to do with me.

"Taylor will help you familiarize yourself," said my mother, who'd finished ordering Lloyd around. "Won't you, Taylor?"

"Oh, sure," I said, not meaning it.

Mom had made the decision, not me. I wasn't going to be introducing this guy to my friends. Not to any of them.

I tuned back in to hear my mother saying, "I'll arrange for you to be enrolled in Taylor's school at the beginning of the week. You'll find it all very unfamiliar, but she'll help you find your feet."

Mom was expecting me to hold this guy's hand on Monday when we went to school? Massive dire! "Oh, sure," I said again, but this time with real sarcasm.

Mom ignored this, continuing with a description of Fysher-Platt Academy and some of the classes he'd be expected to take. Barrett looked pretty stunned at it all. I was pretty stunned too. How was I going to explain to my friends this weird cousin who'd suddenly appeared out of nowhere? I knew what they'd think—that I was related to a dumb farmie. No, thanks!

4 :: Barrett

It was plain my cousin Taylor was unhappy. When I glanced back at her, she was glowering out the window. My aunt was still talking, detailing all the plans she had for me. Apparently I was to have no say in my future. I'd have to endure whatever happened. I told myself as soon as I was legally old enough, I'd go back home. I'd have to wait more than two years, but still, it made me feel better to have a plan in place.

"How can I send messages back to my friends at Simplicity?" I asked, thinking of Jessica. She wasn't officially my girlfriend, but probably would have been soon, if Uncle Paul hadn't died and my aunt hadn't come to take me away.

"Does Simplicity receive mail?"

I shook my head. "We neither receive mail, nor send it."

"How stupid!" said my aunt. "My brother's refusal to use everyday communication systems leads to the ludicrous situation where any letter you write to your friends will have to be delivered by courier at considerable expense.

And I've no idea how you'll get any reply, unless your new leader makes some necessary changes and joins the twenty-first century."

"Leader Renquist won't alter anything. Simplicity will continue exactly as before." A horrible shaft of homesickness and sorrow stabbed me. Maybe I'd never see anyone at Simplicity again.

I glanced over at Aunt Kara. She had a very fine profile, with a strong nose and determined chin. I'd noticed she had very even, very white teeth. Her dark auburn hair was swept back from her face in elaborate waves that seemed frozen in place, like a red helmet.

I wanted to like my aunt, but my only source of information about her had been Uncle Paul, and he'd been very critical of his sister. He maintained that, as head of the influential Ads-4-Life Council, far too much power was concentrated in her hands.

When discussing his sister, Uncle Paul usually came up with the quotation: "As Lord Acton said, 'Power tends to corrupt, and absolute power corrupts absolutely.'"

My uncle's scorn also extended to my aunt's husband, Professor Adrian Stokes, an expert in the psychology of persuasion, or, as Uncle Paul scathingly described it: "An advocate for brainwashing the public until they're little more than buying machines." His face had grown red as he'd continued, "Kara and her disgraceful husband are shameless supporters of marketing, selling, *advertising*."

He always said this last word with particular venom.

"Their activities blight all human society. People's minds are controlled, their willpower sapped. An individual only has the illusion of freedom of choice—everyone is a pitiful, brainwashed consumer, all too willing to be manipulated."

Thinking back, only once could I remember him mentioning Taylor. His mouth had turned down as he'd said, "You have a cousin, the sole offspring Kara and Adrian have managed to produce. Her name is Taylor. It's unlikely you'll ever meet her, but you wouldn't want to waste your time having anything to do with the girl, anyway. She won't have a single original thought in her head. Unlike you, she hasn't had the advantage of a healthy upbringing close to nature, and untainted by the evils of the Chattering World."

I was brought back to the present by a burst of discordant music. Taylor rummaged around in her bag and retrieved a small, bright green object that snapped open in her hand to reveal a little screen and many tiny buttons. As I watched, surprised, the screen expanded to a greater size. From the front seat I could only catch a glimpse of someone's face in it.

"Gabi?... No! Really? You're kidding me! It can't be true!"

"I said no calls," snapped Aunt Kara.

"Hold on, Gabi... Mom, you'll never guess. That feeb new girl at school, Acantha? The one with the frizzy hair? Like, she's made it through to the second round of the

Ugly-D to Teen Queen competition! Would you believe it?"

"Amazing news," said Aunt Kara in a very sarcastic tone, "but you can learn the fascinating details later."

Taylor gave an exaggerated sigh. "Go to text, Gabi. Mom's totally carrying on about me taking calls in the car."

As Taylor began tapping on various buttons, I said to Aunt Kara, "What's *Ugly-D to Teen Queen*?"

"A transformation program. Ugly duckling to swan, with every step of the process shown on television to an audience of millions." She showed her even, white teeth in a broad smile. "Excellent advertising opportunities, particularly for product placement. Thousands of girls will be lining up, hoping to get selected. Countless more will be glued to the screen, watching the program. For companies with the appropriate products, this provides a most desirable teen–young adult demographic."

It was almost unthinkable to contemplate strangers peering into someone's life this way. "How horrible to have no privacy."

My comment amused my aunt. "Privacy is an outdated concept, Barrett. People will do anything to put their intimate selves in front of an audience. It validates them, makes them feel worthwhile."

"These *Ugly-D* girls—why would admitting they believe they're unsightly make them feel worthwhile?"

"Because a sincere interest is taken in the challenges their imperfections present."

"Sincere interest?" Now I was the one being sarcastic.

Aunt Kara waved my comment away. "To be the focus of everyone's attention is very empowering. Not all of us are lucky enough to be good-looking and socially adept, Barrett. Unattractive girls in particular have a hard time. The program provides an opportunity for selected young women to have access to transformation specialists."

I didn't want to hear any more, but I didn't know how to say so without appearing rude. Her voice enthusiastic, Aunt Kara explained how a team of registered experts worked on ten finalists' faces, bodies, attitudes, and social skills.

"Doctors, life stylists, and others who are part of the transformation team become famous as well." My aunt's voice was warmly approving. "And every step will be watched by a huge audience of ready and willing consumers, keen to buy anything they believe will transform them too. At the end of three exciting months, Prince Charming—some minor celebrity, so he won't be too expensive—picks the most beautiful of the ten finalists. The lucky young woman is crowned Transformed Teen Queen. That final program is guaranteed to achieve stratospheric ratings."

"Ratings?"

"Figures indicating comparative audience size. The higher the ratings, the more companies are willing to pay for advertisements in the program."

"So there's one Teen Queen, and all the other girls lose?"

Aunt Kara frowned. "They're much better looking than they were before, so they've gained something very valuable."

I sat back to think about a society where people seemed so willing to have their private lives exposed. I wished I could talk it over with Jessica, or Matthew, or Jane-Marie. It would be so much easier to understand if I could share all this with friends.

Cousin Taylor broke into my thoughts with the announcement she was starving.

"You can't possibly be," said Aunt Kara. "There was ample food at the wake."

"That homemade stuff? Couldn't eat it. Oh, come on, Mom. Look up ahead. There's a Cluck Cluck."

My aunt gave an exasperated sigh, but she turned off the road and joined a line of cars beside a square, purple-and-white building with a huge yellow chicken on the roof. There was a big grin on its beak and its wings were extended like welcoming arms.

Aunt Kara pressed a button and the window beside her slid down. "You want something?" she said to me.

"I'm not sure..." I'd been too upset to eat at Uncle Paul's wake, but I had no idea how this food would taste.

"Everybody loves Cluck Cluck," said Taylor from the back seat.

"All right, then," I said to my aunt. "Thank you."

She leaned out to speak into a small box, also shaped like a smiling chicken.

"Cluck Cluck Special for two," she said.

"Any drinks with that?" inquired a disembodied voice.

"I want a jumbo Octo," came from the back seat.

"Two jumbo Octo-Kolas," said my aunt. "And one medium coffee. Black. No sweetener."

The tinny voice responded in a singsong, "For two, Cluck Cluck Special. The chicken chickens recommend! And two jumbo Octo-Kolas. Eight secret ingredients, eight ways to drinking pleasure with its zesty, besty taste! And one medium Cluck Cluck Premium Coffee. Black. No sweetener. Drive through to the serving window, please."

"Is this fast food?" I asked, having heard of it from my uncle, but only in terms of how the industry threatened the health of the nation. "Obesity! Diabetes! Cancer!" Uncle Paul would bellow. "Lemmings eating their way into an early grave."

My aunt had no such negative view. "Not fast food, Barrett," she said. "The term is rapid restaurant. Food-to-go is an enormous industry, every day supplying millions of nutritious meals to families too busy to worry about cooking for themselves."

We reached the serving window, where a young man in a bright purple uniform, with a cap shaped like a rooster's head, handed over two large purple bags, followed by a slotted tray with two gigantic drink containers and one slightly smaller one branded Cluck Cluck Premium Coffee.

Smiling, he said, "Cluck Cluck greets Ms. Kara Trent's party. We know you have many rapid restaurants to choose from, and we thank you for choosing Cluck Cluck. It is our honor to serve you. Have a truly wonderful day!"

She handed me the bags and drink containers, then took the coffee and placed it in a holder that popped out from the armrest between us. As we drove away, I said, "Isn't he embarrassed to wear that rooster hat?"

"Of course not. No doubt he's proud to be the public face of Cluck Cluck Corporation."

"He knew your name."

My aunt pointed to the bottom of the windscreen. "See the barcode there?"

I peered at the glass. Etched into it, almost invisibly, was a pattern of lines.

"As my vehicle entered the drive-through, a machine read the barcode and immediately identified me. The moment I placed the order, the cost was debited to my account."

"Does it only work with Cluck Cluck?"

My aunt raised her eyebrows. "Good heavens, Barrett, that would hardly be cost-effective. The technology operates for all drive-through facilities. It also automatically pays tolls, parking structure fees, and so on. And the billboards we've been passing? Each vehicle receives different ads. In our case, the barcode would indicate a selection of products suited to the age and lifestyle of the members of my high-income household."

Taylor reached over my shoulder to grab one of the purple bags. "Hand me my Octo-Kola, would you?"

I passed one of the large containers back to her. On it was the illustration of a chicken waving a flag that had the words: You'll love Octo-Kola's zesty besty taste!

Peering into the remaining purple bag, I said, "This doesn't look like any chicken I've seen before."

Aunt Kara was amused. "Of course it doesn't. Paul brought you up eating totally unprocessed food of uneven quality. In contrast, Cluck Cluck Chicken is standardized, tenderized, and reconstituted into palatable, bite-sized portions, with added vitamins and minerals to provide a balanced meal."

I selected a piece of Cluck Cluck Chicken. It didn't taste like anything in particular, just very salty. And it hardly needed any chewing, as it seemed to dissolve into mush in my mouth.

"Good, isn't it?" said my cousin. Incredibly, she seemed to mean it.

"It's all right."

"Try the Octo-Kola."

I took a big sip, thinking its zesty, besty taste couldn't possibly be any more ghastly than the chicken.

It was.

5 :: Barrett

Aunt Kara kept talking about the new life I was to enjoy, apparently not noticing, or not caring, that I had fallen silent. I was dizzy with exhaustion by the time we entered the outskirts of the city. At first I gazed out of the car window with interest, noticing how the houses became larger and more grand as we went towards the center, but after a while everything became a blur of lights and vehicles and buildings. I was both dreading and looking forward to learning more about the Chattering World, but right now all I wanted was somewhere quiet where I could close my eyes and go to sleep.

I must have looked like an open-mouthed idiot when we turned into a driveway and pulled up in front of a two-story mansion, like the grand edifices I'd read about in books. I couldn't believe all these rooms housed just one small family of three. Four now, if you counted me.

A woman opened the huge, brass-studded door before we'd had time to start up the wide sandstone steps.

"Welcome home, Madam."

"Thank you, Eva." She gestured towards me. "Let me introduce my nephew, Barrett. Barrett, this is Eva. She's our live-in housekeeper. We couldn't do without her. She's irreplaceable."

Eva was a tall, angular woman with a pale oval face and large dark eyes. Her narrow skull was covered with tightly curled dark brown hair. She seemed very stern at first, but then she smiled, and her face was illuminated with good humor. I liked her immediately.

"Lloyd called to ask you to prepare the blue suite?" Aunt Kara asked.

"He did." Then she mystified me by asking my aunt, "Do you want it quiescent or activated?"

"Quiescent. Activation can come later."

My cousin Taylor grinned, but when I raised my eyebrows in an unspoken question, she quickly looked away, and I was too tired to ask Aunt Kara what quiescent or activated meant.

Aunt Kara said she had important matters to deal with, and instructed Taylor to give me a quick tour of the house. She didn't look enthusiastic, but complied. First, she took me upstairs to my bedroom, so I could drop off my canvas bag. I hardly had time to take in its extraordinary dimensions before Taylor was off down the hallway. Having the uneasy feeling I'd get lost on my own, I hurried to catch up with her.

I tried to form a mental map of where we'd been, but my tired brain wouldn't cooperate. The rooms were very impressive, but *noisy*. In one, a whole wall had moving pictures, accompanied by sound that seemed to come from all directions at once. In other rooms, music played, machines hummed, devices beeped...

By the time we'd finished, the confusion of jangling noises had left my ears ringing. The contrast with the tranquility at Simplicity was a shock. "Are there any quiet places in the house?" I asked Taylor.

She blinked at me. "Why would you want a quiet place?"

"Don't you find everything very loud?"

Taylor gave me a puzzled look. "Not really."

I suddenly realized she must be so used to continual noise she didn't notice it.

Taylor took me back to my bedroom so I could wash up before dinner. She indicated a little box on the wall. "I'm guessing you don't have air-conditioning at Simplicity," she said, "so you won't know to set the temperature for your room."

"Can't I just open a window?"

She shook her head as though I'd asked the most stupid question in the world, showed me how to adjust the air-conditioning setting, then left me with the admonition that I had thirty minutes before dinner.

I gazed around, never having seen anything like it before. It was clear why Aunt Kara had called it the blue suite: blue was the predominant color. The thick navy carpet contrasted with the pale blue walls and ceiling. The bedspread and curtains had a matching blue-and-white abstract pattern.

Apart from a blue leather lounge chair, all the other furniture was glossy white, and there was a great deal of it. My room at Simplicity had a narrow bed and an upended box beside it on which sat a plain kerosene lamp, the only light source in the room. My clothes and boots had been kept in a curtained alcove in one corner.

Now I had a table on either side of the bed, each holding a large lamp with a blue porcelain base. Over by the window was a round table with a glass top and two white chairs.

I opened the first of two doors to find a walk-in wardrobe, with a tall chest of drawers and hanging space enough for twenty people. My shabby canvas bag was tucked away in the corner. Eva had unpacked my things, and the pitifully small amount of clothing I'd brought huddled at the end of a long bar obviously designed to hang many more items than I possessed. My hand-sewn underwear and my nightshirt had been placed in a drawer. They looked as out of place as I felt.

The other door led to an astonishing bathroom. Everything was glistening: the cream tiles, the shiny gold taps, the mirrored wall that reflected my solemn face back at me. The bath was sunk into the floor, like something in an ancient Roman villa. Behind a frosted glass door, I found a shower.

And there was an indoor toilet. At Simplicity the privies

were situated some way from the living quarters. Of course I'd read of flushing toilets, but never seen one in action. I couldn't resist pushing the button several times to watch the water swirl around the bowl and disappear.

::

Fatigue had really set in by the time Taylor came to collect me for dinner. "My parents have this dumb idea that every day we should always have at least one meal together," she said, leading the way down the stairs. "It's a total drag."

I was used to having breakfast, lunch, and dinner with everyone else in Simplicity's communal hall. Only occasionally, when working on a back paddock, would we take food with us. "Why would you want to eat by yourself?" I asked.

Taylor gave me a pitying look. "There's a thousand things I'd rather be doing than sitting at a table staring at my parents." She gave a discontented sigh. "And like, it's *Saturday*. Any other time I'd be out with my friends, not stuck at home."

She didn't say it, but it was plain that I was the reason she hadn't gone out tonight.

"We think the same way," I said. "You'd rather I wasn't here, and so would I."

"Well... yes." She added quickly, "Not that it's your fault. It's all my mother's idea."

I was touched by a flicker of hope. "Perhaps Aunt Kara will change her mind and let me return to Simplicity."

Taylor opened the dining room door. "Good luck! Mom never changes her mind."

Uncle Adrian hadn't come home yet, so his place was vacant. Aunt Kara came in, poured herself a glass of wine, and sat down. Eva served the meal, then left the room. Obviously she wasn't going to join us. I wondered why that was.

During the evening meal at Simplicity, everyone at each table would share what we had been doing during the day. In silence, Aunt Kara picked up her knife and fork and began to eat. Taylor did the same. The only sound in the room was soft music, which was nothing like the cacophony Taylor seemed to enjoy.

I found the intricate sounds so pleasant I said to Aunt Kara, "That music—I like it."

"It's chamber music played by a string quartet. Bach, Vivaldi. Someone like that. The idea is that soothing rhythms will aid digestion." She turned her attention to my cousin. "You're enrolled in an advanced music appreciation course, Taylor. Why don't you tell us who the composer is?"

Taylor wrinkled her nose. "It's not my kind of music, but it's Handel. His *Water Music Suite*."

Aunt Kara raised one eyebrow. "Impressive. I'm delighted to find you've actually learned something."

My cousin shrugged. End of conversation.

I hardly noticed what was on my plate, just that it was hot and filling. Knowing I should stay awake to meet my uncle, I fought the almost overwhelming desire to close my eyes. I did my best to hide my yawns, but as soon as the meal was over, Aunt Kara told me to go to bed. "You can meet Adrian tomorrow," she said.

Back in my blue room—I surprised myself by finding it without difficulty—I had a quick wash, then fell into the bed. My last thoughts were how soft it was, and how lost I felt.

6 :: Taylor

"Oh, Mom! I was planning to sleep in. You know I never get up early on Sunday mornings."

My mother plunked herself down on the side of my bed. "It's nearly eleven, Taylor. Your cousin's been up since six, I believe."

Oh, great! Now I was going to be compared to a farmie! "Wow, Mom, I'm impressed, but don't expect *me* to get up at the crack of dawn."

Her mouth tightened. "We need to discuss the coming week at school. For Barrett, everything will be strange."

I smothered a yawn. "Can we do this later?"

Bad move. Mom expected everyone, particularly me, to just cave and do whatever she wanted, when she wanted it. Looking impatient, she said, "We do it now."

I sat up and rested my chin on my bent knees. "What's to discuss? Cousin Barrett gets enrolled at Fysher-Platt. End of story."

"I've sent him off with Eva to shop for suitable clothes. He'll also get his own Om."

I smothered another yawn. "Why bother? Who'll call him? His Simplicity friends wouldn't know how."

"*You'll* be able to keep in touch with your cousin when you're not together."

This was totally dire. After all, I hadn't wanted him to come home with us in the first place. "I'm supposed to be his nursemaid, am I?"

Mom's expression turned extra flinty. "This is important, and I'm expecting you to be cooperative, Taylor. Our world is foreign to Barrett. You're to help him cope with unfamiliar situations."

I groaned. "Like that'll be everything." I gave her an imploring look. "This is *so* unfair, Mom. What about my friends? They'll think I'm related to a total bleeb."

She didn't seem to care how embarrassed I was going to be. "He won't be the first person they've met from a farming background."

"But he's not from a farm. He's from a weird cult place. Once Barrett starts raving on about Simplicity, it'll be obvious to everyone that he's really strange. Then what do I say?"

"You'll think of something," she said briskly.

I looked at my mother. She wasn't a cuddly person. Her red hair was the warmest thing about her. Years ago, when I was a little kid, I remembered saying to her, "Do you love me?"

"You're my daughter, so of course I love you," she'd replied.

Perhaps it was true then, and maybe was still true. It was hard to tell—Mom was so self-contained, and didn't show much affection. Right now, she was frowning as she checked her watch. "Your father wants to see you in his study. You've got fifteen minutes to get yourself up and dressed."

This was my mother's idea of getting me to hurry, but I wasn't going to rush. Besides, Dad wouldn't care if I took my time. Unlike Mom, he wasn't a punctuality freak.

After she left, I got out of bed and wandered into my bathroom. My father had had one of the new cylindrical shower alcoves installed for me. I punched in a request for a leisurely shower and hair wash, and stepped into the cylinder, which began to rotate, at the same time blowing bubbling jets of warm water and shower gel. Then a hair-wash helmet came down from the ceiling and massaged my scalp with warm water and shampoo. This was followed by the rinse cycle, followed by jets of warm air to dry my hair and skin. Last, it finished with a fine spray of body lotion. I wasn't sure I liked the shower alcove yet—it made me feel a bit like a utensil in a dishwasher.

Forty minutes later I arrived at Dad's door. He usually dressed really well—he said making a good impression was vital for success—but at home on Sundays he relaxed by wearing the rattiest clothes he could find. Today he had on creased khaki shorts and a faded blue T-shirt.

"How's my girl?" He gave me a hug.

"Great, Dad. Hey, you know it's my birthday soon?"

He looked wary. "Yes...?"

"There's this Resonic Earbud—"

"Fine. Go ahead and get it. Charge it to me."

I kissed his cheek. "You're the best."

Dad's usually a softie with me, but when he tries, he can be a bit scary. Part of it's to do with the fact he's big, with broad shoulders, but mostly it's his thin-lipped mouth and his slate gray eyes. They're paler than mine, and look weird, sometimes, as if there's a machine clicking away inside his head.

"I want something from you in return, Taylor."

It was my turn to look wary. "What?"

"Your mother tells me you're not particularly keen on having Barrett join our family."

Right there, Dad! "I don't think *Barrett's* keen," I said. "It's like he's on another planet. Last night his eyes were practically out on stalks. He'd never even seen an entertainment wall before."

"He'll adjust."

"No chance he's ever going to be happy here." I was extra sincere. "He'd be much better off in that Simplicity place."

I tried to tell myself I was saying this for Barrett's sake, but a little voice in my head sniggered, "Oh, *sure.*"

Dad said, "Your mother and I have talked it over. Barrett is not returning to Simplicity."

Okay, this was going to be difficult, but I could usually get my father to do whatever I wanted. Looking concerned,

I said, "Poor Barrett will be so unhappy. He'll never fit in. It's really cruel, Dad."

He laughed. "Nice try, but just for once, you're not twisting me around your little finger."

"But—"

"No buts. You're to introduce him to your friends. He's to be included in everything you do."

"Oh, that's dire! They'll think I'm a drupe, dragging him along with me." I gave my father my best pleading look. "Come on, Dad, don't ask me to do this."

"It's important, Taylor. Surely your mother has made that clear."

"She thinks everything's important. Oh, *please,* Dad..."

He shook his head. "It's not negotiable. You'll report to me each evening. I'll want to know everything Barrett has done, and where he's been."

"Jeez, aren't you going to put a Safety Sentinel on him anyway? You'll know exactly where he is all the time, without getting *me* involved."

"A GPS Safety Sentinel can't show the range of Barrett's psychological and emotional responses to situations that are alien to him." Dad's tone was the super-reasonable one he always used when he was trying to get someone to go along with what he wanted. I was determined it wasn't going to work on me, at least not this time.

"I can tell you right now how Barrett will be responding," I said. "He'll be wandering around looking surprised. You don't need me to be there."

My father cleared off a chair—his office was always a mess—and sat me down. He found another chair for himself and placed it opposite mine.

Leaning forward in a just-between-you-and-me manner, he said, "I don't think you understand how important this is. Barrett provides an unprecedented opportunity for original research, because he's been entirely untouched by our modern world. His responses are not contaminated by past experiences with, for example, advertising, therefore observing the psychological impact each encounter makes upon him will provide very valuable data, particularly in my field of persuasion."

I folded my arms. "Why do you want me involved, Dad? You can ask him yourself how he feels and what he thinks."

"Personal observation is so much more valuable than having the subject answer questions. I'd like you to observe him very closely when he's encountering anything new to him. Try to be subtle, but ask Barrett how he feels, and what he's thinking." My father put his hand on my arm. "And this is in confidence, Taylor. It's between you, me, and your mother. Barrett is to know nothing about it."

"You're asking me to spy."

Dad grinned. "Don't be melodramatic. It doesn't suit you."

"Why me?" I pouted, knowing I was being childish.

"You're his cousin, and therefore have every reason

to spend time with him. He'll be needing constant guidance."

It was clear I'd lost, but I still made one last attempt to change my father's mind. "Everyone's going to make fun of Barrett. And if I have to stick to him like glue, they'll make fun of me too."

He sighed. "Just for once I'd like you to do something without a full-scale argument."

It was hopeless protesting anymore. "Okay," I said, "but you owe me, Dad. *Big time.* And don't think I won't collect."

My father's thin lips curved in a dry smile. "I have no doubt you will. And that it'll be big time."

::

As soon as I left Dad's office, I called Gabi on my Om. Dad had said it was confidential, but Gabi was my very best friend, so naturally I had to tell her all about it, but only after I'd sworn her to secrecy. I thought at least she'd agree how unfair it was, but Gabi was more interested in Barrett than any problems I might have.

"So what's this country cousin like? Cute?"

I glared at Gabi's face on the screen. "Hey, I'm the one stuck with this guy."

"Yeah, yeah. But what's his name? Barrett? Is he cute?"

"How could he be? He's spent his whole life in this creepy cult place. No chance he's cute."

When Gabi got her teeth into something, she wouldn't

let go. She was like my mother that way. "So what's he look like? Is he tall?"

"I suppose."

"Well, is he or isn't he? Are you telling me he's a midget?"

That made me laugh. "He's no midget. He's taller than me."

In the screen, Gabi grinned. "Everyone's taller than you."

"Ha, ha," I said.

"Make some excuse to get him into the room, so I can look at him over your shoulder."

"Can't. He's off shopping with Eva. Would you believe the only clothes he had were overalls and heavy workboots?"

Gabi wouldn't give up. "Beam me a pic, then."

"I haven't got one. Anyway, you can see for yourself tomorrow." I heaved a sigh. "Would you believe I'm supposed to babysit this guy, like he's some little kid?"

Gabi continued to show an annoying curiosity about my cousin. "Has Barrett got a girlfriend?"

"Not anymore." I told her about Jessica back at Simplicity, and how she'd sobbed when Barrett was leaving.

"I'd cry too, if Nat was going away."

Blonde, blue-eyed Gabi was so good-looking she could have anybody she liked, but recently she'd exchanged bonding bracelets with Nat. He was a big guy with a long, serious face, who spent half his life studying. No fun at all.

Besides, he didn't belong to our group, so I couldn't see why Gabi was so interested in him. I mean, basically he was too boring to live.

"You've got Nat," I said, "so why the questions about my farmie cousin?"

Gabi shrugged. "He sounds interesting."

"Believe me," I said, "he's *not*."

"Maybe you could use him to make Steve jealous."

Gabi knew I was keen on Steve Rox, although he hardly noticed me. Steve was my Uncle Maynard's son. Uncle Maynard wasn't a blood relative, but I called him "uncle" because he'd been a friend of the family since before I was born.

"In a zillion years, Steve wouldn't be jealous of Barrett," I said.

It was more likely, I thought, that Steve would pity me, because I'd been landed with a cousin to cart around.

"Can't wait to meet Barrett," said Gabi.

"Trust me, Gabi, you can wait."

I'd had enough of the subject, so I said, "Tell me about Acantha. Like, what was she wearing at the audition? Something way gleeky?"

"Way gleeky," Gabi agreed. She added, "It's not her fault, though. I was talking with her, and she's really nice. Her parents were plague doctors in Africa before they moved here. She's seen some awful things."

Gabi was always a pushover for a good story, true or not.

"Yeah, yeah," I said. "No matter where Acantha comes from, she's still an outer."

Gabi nodded, but I could see she wasn't convinced.

"Don't go soft on me," I said. "We've got to keep our standards."

She grinned at me. "If your cousin joins our group, won't that lower our standards, right there and then?"

She had a point. Jeez!

7 :: Barrett

Eva took me shopping for new clothes in a much smaller vehicle than the one Aunt Kara had driven the day before. This one was also black, and had the same Ads-4-Life Council words running in a loop around it.

The road was full of other vehicles, and tall buildings were pressing in on every side, crowding out the sky. I wished I could see my own countryside, green and growing. That made me think about Simplicity, and all the questions Taylor's father had asked me this morning when we'd had breakfast together.

I knew Professor Adrian Stokes was an important academic who specialized in the psychology of persuasion, and I'd wondered if I should be formal, and address him as "sir." Aunt Kara was my blood relative, so I felt quite at ease calling her "aunt," but her husband was another matter.

To be on the safe side, when we'd met at the breakfast table, I'd said, "Good morning, sir."

He'd smiled. "Uncle Adrian will do."

He was a big, dark-haired man, with large, soft hands and opaque gray eyes. His most notable feature, I thought, was his chin, which was large and square, rather like a shovel blade. He'd watched me intently as I answered the same questions Aunt Kara had raised when she'd first met me yesterday.

At last I'd said, "Why are you asking me all this?"

He'd shown his very white teeth in a smile that seemed forced, as though he didn't mean it. "It fascinates me, Barrett. You personify the concept of the noble savage, untouched by civilization."

"Do you mean Rousseau's idea of the noble savage? Or John in Huxley's *Brave New World*?"

Uncle Adrian had looked startled for a moment, and then amused. "Kara told me Paul had emphasized literature in your education. I imagine you're better read than I, as far as the classics are concerned."

Now, sitting in the car, it came to me that when I'd been shown around the house last night, there were no bookshelves. "Eva," I said, "do you read books?"

"Whenever I can find the time, although some may not look like the books you're used to." She glanced over at me with a slight smile. "I won't even try to explain what an e-book is. You'll see one soon enough at school."

The mention of school made my stomach turn over, so I tried to concentrate on something else. "May I ask you a question?"

"You can ask. I may not have the answer."

"Why do Aunt Kara and Uncle Adrian have different surnames?"

"When they married, your aunt simply decided not to take her husband's name."

"So what is Taylor's?" I asked. "I'm guessing it must be a combination, either Stokes-Trent or Trent-Stokes."

"Your cousin's name is Taylor Trent. Your Aunt Kara insisted on this, to carry on her family's name."

I thought about how I was carrying on the Trent name myself, as the last male in the line.

Something else had been bothering me. "I have another question," I said.

Eva looked amused. "Go on."

"When I met Aunt Kara and Taylor yesterday, Taylor said people don't shake hands anymore, because of what she called the Plagues. But you shook hands with me when we met."

With a derisive snort for emphasis, Eva said, "The whole idea that deadly diseases will spread by simply shaking hands is a complete overreaction encouraged by the media, who pump up sensational stories, and the companies manufacturing antibacterial and antiviral products." She shook her head. "As if we all weren't paranoid enough already!"

"So there are no Plagues?"

"Oh, they exist, all right, but mainly in poor countries. Now and then travelers come back infected, but they're put in isolation wards and treated with the latest drugs.

Of course the media love to focus on sensational stories of thousands dying in foreign places from deadly viruses like Q-Plague, so it's not surprising people get hysterical about the subject."

"So nobody dies here from these foreign diseases?"

Her expression grew serious. "The health authorities don't like to admit it, nor do the drug companies, but there are a few diseases for which there's no effective treatment at all. So far we've been lucky, as our strict quarantine laws have prevented any large-scale outbreaks."

"But it could happen?"

"There's always a chance." She added sardonically, "And if, say, Q-Plague did break out, the media would want the biggest disaster possible, with a death toll spiraling out of control."

"Why?" I asked, astonished. "Why would anyone want people dead?"

"The more shocking the news, the larger the audience. The larger the audience, the more advertisers clamor to place their advertisements where potential customers will be exposed to them."

Uncle Paul had particularly stressed the role of the media in his condemnation of the Chattering World, reserving his harshest remarks for television. In my imagination I could see his scornful face as he said, "Television deliberately cripples the critical skills of its audience by consistently appealing to emotions, rather than intellect."

The blast of an impatient horn jerked me back to the present. We were driving through streets crammed with vehicles, most of them with brightly illuminated panels or with words constantly running in a loop along the sides like our car.

The rear window of the vehicle in front of us was filled with constantly changing pictures of people running, pedaling bicycles, swimming, lifting weights, and so on. *Health! Strength! Vigor! Social Success! Contact your nearest Feelgood Fitness Center today!* flashed in brilliant orange letters.

"I've never been shopping before," I said. "I'm not sure what to expect."

"It's a major pastime for some." Eva's voice was dry. "Taylor, for example, loves shopping for clothes."

"That's all we're doing today? Getting clothes for me?"

"And an Om."

"That's the device Taylor had. What exactly is it?"

"An essential to modern living," said Eva. "Its brand name is OmniDrive, usually shortened to Om."

"Omni is a prefix meaning all," I said, remembering Uncle Paul's insistence that effective education must always include a rigorous study of the English language and its history.

Eva looked at me approvingly. "Exactly. An OmniDrive has multiple functions. It operates as a telephone, plays music, receives and sends email, records voice messages, shoots and displays photographs and videos. You can also view a movie on your Om, or play any number of interactive video games."

Our line of cars suddenly stopped. I could see red lights ahead, and recognized them from my reading as a form of traffic control. My attention was caught by the huge moving image of a half-naked woman dancing on the blank side of a tall building. Apart from the paintings and statues I'd studied for art history, I'd never seen a woman wearing so little clothing.

I felt myself blush, and looked away. "What's she advertising?"

"Herself," said Eva. "Her name's Petunia Madison."

"You know her?"

"Not personally. Basically, she's famous for being famous," said Eva with a sarcastic smile. "No discernible talent, but that didn't prevent her from getting to the finals of *Worldsong*."

Realizing this meant nothing to me, she added, "*Worldsong*'s an ongoing talent quest shown worldwide on television. It's people's choice—votes come in from the public, and the contestants with the highest scores go on to the grand finale and the chance to win millions of dollars. Rumors are still circulating about vote rigging of the competition."

"So Petunia Madison won?"

"No, she was runner-up to the ultimate winner."

Ahead, lights turned green. Someone, impatient, pounded a horn several times. The traffic started moving again, and I lost sight of the wall and the dancing woman.

"Why would she be advertising herself?" I asked.

Eva gave a derisive grunt. "The young woman's had a taste of fame and found it intoxicating. She doesn't want to slip from public view, so she advertises herself, hoping for a movie or TV offer."

"But you said she had no talent."

"Barrett, in this world you don't always need to have talent to be famous. And most people, once they taste fame, don't want to give it up. Staying in the public eye is the hard part because so many others are fighting for the spotlight."

A huge collection of brightly colored buildings loomed on our right.

"Shoppaganza," said Eva. "Our destination." Now I could see Shoppaganza Complex spelled out in gigantic fiery letters above the structures.

Abruptly Eva turned off the street and we plunged down a steep incline. "Where are we going?" I asked, horribly aware that we were now underground.

"Parking."

In a moment, we were zipping along rows and rows of parked vehicles. "Watch for a space," Eva said.

"There," I said, pointing. Another driver coming the opposite way saw the vacant space too.

Eva chuckled as she swung into it, cutting off the other car. "Mall wars," she said, as the driver indignantly thumped his horn.

Before Eva could turn off the ignition, a panel in the wall in front of the car lit up, and a succession of moving pictures appeared, one after the other, detailing the attractions of Shoppaganza Complex.

"Are there advertisements *everywhere?*" I said.

"Everywhere," she said with a smile. "These ones will turn off as soon as the sensors detect we've moved away."

I got out, feeling as though I was in an artificial cave and the ceiling might collapse at any moment and crush me into oblivion. Looking at the hundreds of parked vehicles around us, I said, "How will we ever find this car again?"

"Trust me," said Eva. "I haven't lost one yet. If I forget where I've parked"—she held up the black rectangular card she'd used instead of an ignition key to start the car—"this has been imprinted with the signature of the location. As soon as we entered the parking space, it sent a wireless message to this keycard. When we leave the space, the message will be removed."

She handed me the black card. "Hold it close to your mouth, say 'vehicle location' and see what happens."

I followed her instructions and *Parking Level Two: Space 205* glowed in fluorescent red letters on the black background.

We joined other people heading towards a bright sign scrolling the words: *Your Shoppaganza Experience starts here!*

Immediately we entered, a cacophony of music and raised voices and the shuffle of many feet crashed down on me. And smells—sharp scents and perfumes, greasy food, strange aromas I couldn't identify. And people! Masses and masses of people moving restlessly in all directions, talking to each other or into Oms or in some cases to no one at all, as far as I could see. People were eating, looking into windows, darting into doorways leading to displays of clothes and countless other devices, of which I could only guess the purpose.

Eva strode boldly into the throng. I hurried to keep up. To lose sight of her gaunt figure would leave me alone in a sea of strangers, and I had no idea how to get back to Aunt Kara's place.

As I looked around, I became aware of individuals in the crowd. They all seemed subtly wrong to me. It was their hair and clothes and loud voices. Peering more closely, I saw that most of them had what I assumed were product names somewhere on their clothing. Some even seemed to literally be walking advertisements, because they had colored images and names flickering across their chests or backs, as though the material of their clothing was somehow a screen.

From the stares I was getting, I was as strange to them as they were to me. My hair was longer than that on any of the males I saw, but it was my overalls and boots that made me really stand out.

Ahead, Eva disappeared through a doorway above

which scintillated the silver words: The Maximum Male. I rushed to follow, almost running into her where she'd halted just inside the entrance to survey the store.

The place was much larger than I'd expected, and even more confusing than outside. Loud music with a strange, insistent beat blasted out; multiple screens flashed pictures; disembodied voices frantically boomed promises to provide the latest thing at the best possible price.

There was clothing everywhere: on racks, folded on shelves, arranged on tables. And the colors! Dazzling shades of blue and red and pink and orange...

I jumped when a life-sized dummy near me suddenly turned its head and smiled. Then it said in a deep voice, "Welcome to The Maximum Male, the premier store for everything masculine." It spread its arms wide. "Examine the leisure suit I am wearing. It is an exclusive Philippe Renoir leisure suit, as worn by mega-star Owen Ranstatt in his latest action feature, *Thrillkiller Kill IV.* "

It was eerie, the way the dummy's glowing eyes seemed to actually be looking at me. It went on, "Notice the freedom of movement, the soft texture, the clean, body-enhancing lines." After a pause, it declared, "This Philippe Renoir leisure suit would look very good on you."

I doubted that. The suit was made of some shiny black material and was skintight. The words Philippe Renoir appeared across the chest. The suit had a high neck, sleeves ending just below the elbow and pants stopping just below the knee. The dummy also wore blood red canvas shoes with thick black soles. The word Snaplock flashed on and off along the side of the sole.

"Buy now," said the dummy persuasively, "and gain a wonderful ten percent discount on this Philippe Renoir leisure suit, when purchased with matching Supreme Comfort underwear." It was silent for a moment, then continued with enthusiasm, "Or, today only, we offer an astonishing fifteen percent discount if you include the Philippe Renoir leisure suit, the Supreme Comfort underwear, *and* trend-of-the moment Snaplock shoes."

"I don't want anything like that," I said to Eva, indicating the dummy, which had lost interest in me and had now swiveled its head towards another potential customer. "Welcome to The Maximum Male..." it began.

Eva wrinkled her narrow nose. "Cheap stuff," she said. "My instructions are to buy you the best. The management has already been informed of our requirements, so the next step is to get your physioparas entered."

"Good morning," said a voice suffused with pleasure. "My name is Assistant Quent." The man was dressed entirely in black. Across his chest the name of the shop appeared in silver letters. Underneath this was his name. "My mission is to assist you in any way possible to ensure your visit to The Maximum Male is a premier buying experience. My warmest welcome to the Trent-Stokes Account. If you'll just come this way..."

"How did he know my aunt and uncle's names?" I murmured to Eva.

"We were scanned as soon as we entered." She raised her left hand to reveal a thin bracelet around her wrist. "The machine read the electronic tag and identified me as a person authorized to use the Trent-Stokes account. It also read our requirements for today's shopping in this store."

I shook my head. Everything about this world confused me. I doubted if I would ever understand it.

A few minutes later, I found myself standing inside a metal cylinder while lines of light in grid patterns played over me. The cylinder snapped open and Assistant Quent motioned for me to step out.

He gazed into a flat, brightly lit panel, spread his fingers as though gesturing to the screen, and waited until it beeped at him. "Excellent," he said.

He turned to Eva, who was sitting in one of the soft, comfortable chairs that lined one side of the room. An open door showed a small mirrored cubicle I assumed was a changing area. On the opposite side, the facing wall had a black, glassy surface. "We're ready to proceed," he announced.

"Please do so," said Eva, frowning. "We have other shopping to complete. You now have Barrett's measurements, so the correct size for each item should be waiting for him to try on."

Her impatient tone got immediate action. The assistant hurried to the slick black wall and made an elaborate hand gesture. This clearly activated some control, because a square opening suddenly gaped as part of the wall slid open. I could see what seemed like hundreds of items of clothing, some neatly folded, others hanging on a rack that, as I watched, slowly protruded into the room.

"Not everything there is for me, surely!" I exclaimed, eyeing clothing in every imaginable color. There seemed every chance I would shortly resemble a walking rainbow.

"You must have suitable clothing for tonight," said Eva.

"Why tonight?"

Eva raised her eyebrows. "You weren't told that Senator Maynard Rox and his son, Steve, are to be guests at dinner?"

Quent looked very impressed. "Senator Rox," he murmured.

"No one said anything to me. Perhaps I'm not expected to be there," I said.

Eva gave a dry laugh. "In many ways you're the guest of honor."

"Wait a minute," I said. "He's called *Senator* Rox? Like in ancient Rome?"

This amused Eva and scandalized Quent, who said stiffly, "Senator Rox is a wonderful man—an elected member of the government. Of the Senate, actually. He's at liberty to call himself 'Senator'."

Eva said coolly, "We're not here to discuss politics."

Quent looked flustered for a moment, then collected himself to look with disfavor at my heavy boots. "Perhaps we should start with footwear."

Clearly entertained by my despondent expression, Eva said, "It's not as bad as all that, Barrett. I know it's all new to you, but believe me, many people actually enjoy choosing new clothes."

"I won't be one of them," I said. "Ever."

8 :: Taylor

I was texting Lorena while talking to Gabi on the phone when Mom put her head around the door to say I was supposed to be getting ready for dinner, and I wasn't to be late because Senator Rox would be arriving soon. Like, that was big news? He dropped into our place so often he practically lived here.

"Hold on, Gabi... Mom, do I *have* to be there? Uncle Maynard will understand if you tell him I've got urgent homework."

"Wear that turquoise dress. It looks nice on you."

"It makes me look stupid. I hate it." And I did. My mother had picked it out and insisted on buying it on one of the rare occasions when she'd gone shopping with me. How would she have any idea what sort of clothes I wanted to wear?

"Don't speak to me in that tone, Taylor."

I felt the temperature in my bedroom drop a few degrees. "Sorry," I said, trying to sound as if I meant it.

"Maynard is very keen to meet Barrett," Mom said.

I was beginning to feel a little bit sorry for my cousin. I imagined everyone had stared at him when he'd gone shopping dressed in his overalls and heavy boots. And now Uncle Maynard was coming to look him over as if Barrett was the latest oddity from the bush. "All the more reason why you don't need me there, Mom. Uncle Maynard will be concentrating on Barrett."

"Perhaps your enthusiasm for dinner will be greater if you know that Maynard's bringing Steve with him."

"Steve? Why didn't you say so before?"

Coldly amused, my mother said, "You'll be sitting between Steve and Barrett."

My mood took a nosedive. Steve would take one look at Barrett and laugh. And what would he think of me, having a cousin who belonged to some weird cult that tried to live like people did a hundred years ago?

"Did you hear?" I asked Gabi as soon as Mom left.

"Every word. Wish I could be there. Sounds like it's going to be fun."

Easy for Gabi to say.

::

Dinner wasn't until 8:15 and I was starving, so I went down to the kitchen to get a quick snack. When someone important like Uncle Maynard came to dinner, my parents didn't rely on Eva, but called caterers in to handle the whole thing, so the place was full of strangers rushing around. And, of course, Uncle Maynard's bodyguard was checking everything out, on the faint chance there might be some major danger lurking in our kitchen. I remember asking Mom why Uncle Maynard needed a bodyguard. She'd said people like him in the public eye often received death threats. Most of these were just hot air, but there was always the chance of real danger.

Everyone called the bodyguard by his first name, Will. When in the past I'd asked him what his full name was, he'd smiled and said, "Will will do."

"Will Will Do's your name?" I'd said, joking.

He was a large guy, I suppose like any bodyguard should be, with broad shoulders and a thick neck. Maybe he'd played football a lot, or gone in for weight-lifting in a big way. Otherwise he was quite good-looking, although he wore his sandy hair a bit too short, and his nose seemed to have been broken somewhere along the line.

I gave Will a wave as I dodged around a woman carrying a loaded tray. I was heading for the refrigerator, but had to wait my turn as several people were putting things in or taking them out.

"Hello, Princess," said Will.

I replied, like I always did, "My name's Taylor."

"I know, Princess, I know."

During a pause in the catering action, I grabbed a yogurt out of the fridge. "You need plastic," I said to Will. "If you had your nose fixed, you'd be almost handsome."

"Surgery? No way." He tapped his nose. "Part of the package. Meant to intimidate."

"Doesn't intimidate me."

Will grinned at me. "What could, Princess, I wonder?"

"Taylor!" My mother swanned across the kitchen. She took the yogurt from me and put it back in the fridge. "You're to join your father and Senator Rox in the study. Now."

"What about Steve? I thought he was coming tonight."

"I left Steve and Barrett entertaining each other."

I could imagine how well *that* was going down.

Mom focused on Will. She gave him one of those quick, electric smiles she used on people when she wanted them to do something for her.

"Will, would you mind accompanying Taylor to my husband's study?"

Will took my arm. "Come on, Princess."

Once out of the kitchen, I shook myself free. "I don't need to be accompanied anywhere," I said. "And don't call me Princess."

"What would you prefer? Empress, perhaps? Queen? Monarch of all you survey?"

Will was laughing at me, but I found I didn't really mind. Not that I was interested in him. He was too old, probably in his thirties, but I was guessing that even so, he might be fun to spend time with.

"What do you do in your spare time?" I asked.

Will stopped at the door of Dad's study. "I don't have any," he said. "Guarding Senator Rox is a 24/7 job."

He knocked, then opened the door and ushered me in.

Will didn't come into the room, but stepped back into the hall and shut the door behind him.

Uncle Maynard leaped up and came over to me. As I always did, I noticed how his heavy black eyebrows contrasted with the near white of his hair. He wasn't very tall, but he had so much energy and enthusiasm that somehow he never seemed as short as he was. "Taylor!" He gave me a big hug and a kiss on the cheek. "You look wonderful tonight."

"Thanks."

Naturally I wasn't wearing the turquoise thing Mom wanted me to put on, otherwise he wouldn't have been able to say I looked wonderful. Though, when I thought about it, Uncle Maynard was always telling people how great they looked, no matter what. And smiling. He was always smiling.

"Maynard's a politician to the bone," my father had once remarked. "He's forever selling himself." It was the most critical thing I'd ever heard him say about Uncle Maynard, and I remember my mother had looked sharply at him. Maybe she had a word with him later, because Dad never said anything like that again.

I glanced at my father, who was sitting behind his desk. His slate gray eyes looked back at me. He had a nothing expression on his face, like he wasn't really there.

"Come and sit down, Taylor," said Uncle Maynard, indicating the seat next to him. "I have something confidential to discuss with you."

"I expect it's about Barrett."

He seemed surprised. "Why do you say that?"

I shrugged. "Just that my farmie cousin seems to be the main topic of conversation around here."

"Yes, it *is* about Barrett. I'm sure you realize how rare it is to find someone who's never been exposed to all the wonders of our modern civilization."

"Uh-huh." My father frowned at me. "Yes, Uncle Maynard," I said, ultra polite.

"I know your parents have asked you to spend as much time with your cousin as possible, at least during these first weeks. I must emphasize how important this is, my dear." He patted my hand. "We need your input."

"I can't go *everywhere* with him," I pointed out with a bit of a smile. My father frowned again. Uncle Maynard laughed.

"I certainly don't expect you to accompany your cousin to the bathroom, but whenever possible, I would ask that you try to be with him, just for the next few weeks."

Oh, this was *dire*. With Uncle Maynard demanding I do this as well, there was no way I could get out of it. "Okay," I said, "but I don't understand why."

"Look upon it as a scientific experiment," he said. "It's a once-in-a-lifetime opportunity to observe how someone entirely untouched by our modern world reacts when presented with something alien to his past experiences. And it's important, of course, that Barrett does not realize you are watching him closely."

I couldn't see the big deal. As I'd said to Dad, my cousin could easily be tagged so that there'd be a constant GPS record of where he was. And when I thought about it, there were also tiny medical implants that were used to register vital signs. Couldn't these provide enough feedback?

"Barrett will be wearing a Safety Sentinel that'll show where he is all the time," I said. "If you fit him with a medical monitor too, you'll get all his physical responses. You don't need me."

"Listen to me, Taylor," said Uncle Maynard, his face stern. "Your father's research projects into the psychological aspects of persuasion are highly regarded, and rightly so. His findings have been very influential in advertising, for example. Your mother's Ads-4-Life Council has materially benefited from his conclusions."

I didn't mean to, but I gave a little sigh. Uncle Maynard chuckled. "Boring you, am I? Well, I'll try to be brief. Barrett is a blank slate as far as advertising and other forms of persuasion are concerned. Studying closely how he responds to this new world around him will provide valuable insights into which techniques and strategies work best on a young mind."

I didn't need to ask why Uncle Maynard was so interested. He was one of the main government supporters of Mom's Ads-4-Life Council. Besides, at school my English teacher, Mr. Dunne, had discussed how politicians sold themselves to the public using the same tactics that advertisers used to sell products. That pretty well described Uncle Maynard, so I guessed he'd be keen to know about the latest research.

"I told Dad I'd do it, and I will."

Uncle Maynard beamed at me. "You won't be sorry. In fact, I think you'll find there'll be a nice reward for you at the end."

"What sort of reward?" I asked, thinking how Dad, and now Uncle Maynard, wanted to give me something for keeping an eye on my cousin. It was going to be a total drag, but at least it might turn out to be worthwhile.

"We'll discuss that later, but in the meantime, give some thought to something you'd really like."

"That'd be great."

I looked over at Dad, who was stony-faced, then back to Uncle Maynard, who was still smiling approvingly. I felt an odd twinge of guilt about Barrett. Not that I owed my cousin anything, but there was something nasty about the way he was being set up, all unknowing, like an animal in a lab experiment.

9 :: Barrett

When Aunt Kara introduced me to Steve Rox, I automatically went to shake hands with him. He examined my extended fingers as though they were something he'd never seen before, then said, with close to a sneer, "You'll have to learn our customs. We don't shake hands anymore."

"Barrett's on a steep learning curve," said my aunt. "Right now, most things are foreign to him. Isn't that true, Barrett?"

I agreed it was.

"Then I'll leave you two together. Steve, I'm sure you'll be happy to give Barrett some hints about Fysher-Platt. He'll be enrolling tomorrow."

She left us alone in the small sitting room. There was an awkward silence, at least on my side. Steve looked bored, digging his hands into his pockets and slumping down on one of the fat leather chairs.

"Entertain me," he said. "Tell me about this bizarre little place you come from."

Steve Rox had a stocky build, with thickly muscled

shoulders and large hands. He had light hair and the type of fair skin that burns easily in the sun. I supposed he was dressed in the latest fashion. He wore tight, bright blue pants and a tailored white jacket. The outfit Eva had selected for me was similar, although I'd refused to have it so closely fitted, and had insisted on a dark gray shade.

"I don't imagine you're the slightest bit interested in Simplicity Center," I said mildly.

He narrowed his eyes. "You want some advice, Trent? Keep your head down. And don't cross me."

At Simplicity we never used surnames. In fact, I'd almost forgotten mine was Trent. "Call me Barrett," I said.

"That would mean we were friends, Trent, and I can't see that happening. Not in my lifetime."

I couldn't work out what had caused this animosity. The charitable view was that I was different, and this unsettled him. More realistically, Steve Rox was arrogant, and felt superior to me. There were a few like him at Simplicity—bullies at heart, who leaned on anyone they thought to be weaker.

"Are we to be adversaries, then?" I inquired.

He sat up, scowling. "What?"

"Adversaries. Enemies. Foes."

Eva interrupted whatever Steve was about to say. Dressed elegantly all in black, she swept through the door carrying a silver tray with a crystal decanter and matching glasses. I recognized them from photographs. We had nothing like that at Simplicity.

"I thought you boys might be thirsty," she said.

As I took the tray from her, Steve asked, "Is it wine?"

Amused, she said, "I'm sorry to disappoint you, but it's cider."

Steve made a sound of disgust, and threw himself back into the chair. Eva glanced at me with a quizzical expression on her angular face. I gave a slight shrug. It was going to be a long evening.

::

Dinner was served in a much grander room than the one in which I'd eaten last night. There was a huge black marble fireplace, and even though it wasn't cold, a fire burned behind a brass screen. Above the mantelpiece was a portrait in oils of my aunt and uncle: Aunt Kara was sitting, ankles neatly crossed; Uncle Adrian stood behind her. Both stared out of the frame with aloof, cool expressions.

Senator Maynard Rox came over to greet me, smiling broadly. It was as if he'd known me for years. "Well, Barrett, I hope you're settling in well."

Reminding myself not to try shaking hands, I said, "Yes, sir, thank you."

He clapped me on the shoulder. "You must call me 'Senator' or 'Uncle Maynard,' whichever you prefer. Now that you've joined Kara and Adrian's lovely family, I expect we'll be seeing a lot of each other. If there's anything I can do to help you, just ask."

The senator had a booming bass voice, too big for his body. He was shorter than me, and much more slightly built. Some of his meager height came from his thick, pale hair, which sprang from his scalp like a crest. His eyebrows seemed oddly dark and I noticed his ever present smile didn't reach his washed-out blue eyes.

At that moment, for no reason at all, I recalled a line from Shakespeare: *That one may smile, and smile, and be a villain.*

Abruptly, Senator Rox's smile was switched off, and his face became solemn. "Kara tells me your uncle was tragically killed by a lightning strike. Please accept my deepest condolences."

"Thank you."

The smile was back again as he turned to my aunt. "Kara, I swear you look more beautiful every day. I don't know how you do it. Adrian's a lucky man."

Uncle Adrian didn't look as though he thought himself lucky. His expression was almost bleak. "Perhaps we should take our seats," he said tonelessly.

I wondered what had made him unhappy. Maybe he didn't like the way Senator Rox was complimenting Aunt Kara. Or perhaps the tension I sensed was between Uncle Adrian and my aunt. Whatever the reason, no one else seemed to notice his severe demeanor.

Eva's duty was to usher us to the correct chairs. Each place at the circular glass table was set with more knives, forks, and spoons than I knew what to do with, so I was grateful to Eva when she bent over me to whisper, "Start at the outside and work your way in."

Once we were all seated, Aunt Kara was on my left, Taylor to my right, then came Steve Rox, Uncle Adrian, and Senator Maynard Rox. In the middle of the table was an elaborate flower arrangement and several lit candles in silver holders.

Two of the catering staff, dressed entirely in black like Eva, began to serve the first course, which was made up of several types of melon cut into tiny pieces and covered with very thin slices of some sort of salty meat. I watched which cutlery others picked up, and did the same.

Senator Rox was laughing with Aunt Kara about a recent advertising campaign that had been incredibly expensive to produce, but had failed to persuade many to buy the item. It seemed to be some kind of anti-aging potion for men called Valiant Surprise.

Beside me, I was suddenly conscious that my cousin was looking me over. "You've had your hair cut," said Taylor, who hadn't seen me all day. "It looks mega better."

I preferred it the way it had been, so didn't agree with her, but I said thank you anyway.

"And you've ditched the overalls. That's good."

"Overalls?" said Steve, raising his eyebrows. "You're into overalls, Trent? How very farmie that is."

Senator Rox obviously caught his son's last words. He beamed across the table. Apparently almost everything delighted him. "Barrett comes from a farming community," he said, "but it's nothing like the huge, company-owned agriculs we're used to, Steve. He'll have a lot to teach us about hands-on farming."

"Oh, yeah? Can't wait."

"Tomatoes?" I said to Steve, leaning forward to talk past Taylor.

"Tomatoes? What about them?" He was glaring at me suspiciously, as though I might be mocking him, which I was, of course.

"Your father mentioned hands-on farming. I was offering to show you how to grow tomatoes. It's one of my strengths, tomato growing."

I noticed Taylor hiding a grin. Uncle Adrian's severe expression disappeared and he actually laughed aloud. "He's having a joke at your expense, Steve."

"Sure. I know that," he snapped.

The conversation around the table then turned to another topic—the upcoming elections. Steve took the opportunity to get to his feet and step past Taylor's chair to mine. He bent over to hiss in my ear. "I told you to watch out, Trent. Now I'll have to teach you a lesson. One you won't forget."

Taylor, frowning, put a hand on his arm. "Steve..."

I felt a warm moment of gratitude, that she was defending me... until she added, "Please sit down. Mom *hates* it if anyone stands up during dinner."

10 :: Taylor

I hate Mondays at the best of times, but this one was shaping up to be worse than usual. First, Mom insisted we all have breakfast together. Dire! Dad ducked out by saying he had to leave early for work, which left Mom, me, and Barrett looking at each other over the table.

Second, Mom insisted on driving Barrett and me to Fysher-Platt. My suggestion that she take him with her, but let me meet up with my friends like I usually did before school, got a definite no before I'd even finished asking. Typical!

Mom had her usual toast and black coffee, but she got Eva to cook us a proper breakfast. While my mother checked her busy schedule on her Om, I half watched *Welcome the Morning* newsmagazine. Tad Fortune was a presenter I particularly liked. All the girls did—he was so cool reading the news, but even more so when he was selling Gargantuan handheld computers, and making jokes about how they were super tiny, so their name was bigger than they were.

Thinking that I might as well start earning my promised spying rewards, I said to Barrett, "What do you think about *Welcome the Morning*?" He gazed at me blankly, so I pointed at the TV. "It's the highest rating newsmagazine."

He shrugged. "I wasn't watching."

This was totally hopeless. Tad Fortune's smiling face filled the screen, but today even a sexy guy wasn't enough to keep my mind off the disaster of a day that was waiting for me, so I flicked off the screen and turned my attention to Barrett. I was going to be saddled with him at school and, worse, Steve had made it plain last night he didn't think much of my cousin, and everyone listened to Steve. He'd make fun of Barrett, and our crowd would join in.

So far this morning, Barrett had said about two words to me and Mom, then gone silent. And he was just pushing things around on his plate and hardly eating anything. Remembering how I felt one time when I'd changed schools and been surrounded by strangers, I felt sorry for him, so I said, "It won't be too bad, you know. Just a bit strange for a while."

He looked up and gave me a slight smile. "Thanks."

I looked him over. At least I wouldn't be totally embarrassed to be seen with him today. Eva had done a good job. Barrett's hair had been cut and styled, and he was wearing decent clothes and shoes. He actually was quite handsome, in his own way.

"Did Eva get you an Om?" I asked.

"Yes, but I've got no idea how to work it."

My mother looked up from her own Om. "Weren't the functions explained to you, Barrett?"

"The salesman went through what the device could do, but I have to confess I didn't really grasp most of what he said."

Mom frowned. She was always impatient when people didn't pick up things right away. "Eva should have taken you through it again."

Hearing this, Eva clashed some pans together and mumbled something, probably rude. I hid a smile. I'd always liked the way she stood up to my mother. No one else ever did.

Mom was off in her lecture mode. "Your personalized Om," she said to Barrett, "combines your address book and your schedules, plus telephone, voice recording, radio, digital music player, video player, camera, global positioning, email, and text messaging services. Your Om will coordinate your appointments, organize your travel plans, ensure you receive the latest advertising offers tailored to your needs, and pay for any purchases you might make."

Barrett put up his chin. He looked so determined I wondered for a moment if he was going to pick a fight with my mother, but all he said was, "I don't have any funds, Aunt Kara. As it is, I'm not sure how I can repay you for the clothes and—"

"Repayment isn't necessary," she said, interrupting him before he could finish. "I've arranged for you to have access to a monthly allowance for your personal needs."

"Thank you, Aunt Kara, but—"

He broke off when Mom made an irritated gesture. "Naturally it will be costly to outfit you with all the items you so conspicuously lacked at Simplicity, but you're not to worry about the expense. You're a member of our family now."

Barrett didn't look too happy to hear this, and I agreed with him. He *wasn't* a member of the family, no matter what Mom said. He was a stranger who just happened to be related to us. He said he wanted to go back to his dreary farmie life, and I made a silent promise to help him do just that.

"You have a dentist's appointment today, Barrett. You will spend the morning at Fysher-Platt, and then Eva will pick you up at lunchtime," my mother announced. "That will take the better part of the afternoon, so tomorrow you'll start your first full day of lessons."

Great! Enrolling should take Barrett most of the morning, then he'd be off to the dentist's. That meant after school I could join my friends at Ruby & Jake's Cyberparlor without having to worry about Barrett tagging along.

Ruby & Jake's was *the* place to go after school. There was coffee, of course, plus every other drink you could think of—but no alcohol, at least not officially. And there was music, loud music. The basement held antique arcade games from the last century. Best of all, there were link-ups to other cyberparlors so you could join a whole network of interactive role-play games. Mom would kill me if she found out, but I'd joined Slaughter Quest, using the name Gorgeous Gloria of Thalia. My screen image had been built up from pics Gabi took of me where I looked older and a bit mysterious.

If you knew who to ask, at Ruby & Jake's you could get different flavors of jolters. I didn't do any of the really heavy drugs, couldn't if I wanted to, because my parents had the latest Chemscan machine, but so far jolters, which were milder, weren't detectable. I'd tried some pastel ones, and they'd been okay, but Steve was at me to try purple, which everyone who'd tried it said was way hectic. He'd whispered to me last night that he was getting a delivery of purple today, and we'd made a date to meet in the basement of the cyberparlor after school.

I was always pretty careful not to get home too late on weekdays. I didn't want my parents to ask search-ing questions about what I'd been doing. Of course they thought they knew exactly where I was, but they had no clue. Ruby & Jake's sold a GPS displacer that changed the signal so that the Safety Sentinel showed me as being somewhere else—usually Gabi or Lorena or Candell's place, because we all covered for each other.

I tuned back in to find Barrett asking Mom why he had to go to the dentist. He'd better learn fast that you didn't challenge her instructions and expect to get anywhere.

"You need your teeth checked," she said in a don't argue tone. "I don't imagine you had any form of dental care at Simplicity."

Barrett looked really insulted. "Why would you imagine that, Aunt Kara? A dentist came from the nearest town at least twice a year, and more often if someone had a toothache."

"Nevertheless, you'll keep your appointment this afternoon. Dr. Selkirk is an excellent cosmetic dentist who will correct any problems you have."

"I don't believe I have any problems to be corrected."

Barrett could be right. When he'd smiled I couldn't help noticing how good his teeth were, which was surprising, considering the totally backward place he'd come from.

Mom's expression had gone icy cold. Danger sign! To head off a nasty scene, I said, "Hey, Barrett, what's the harm in having a checkup? I have one regularly. Dr. Selkirk'll look in your mouth, say everything's fine, and that'll be it."

That got me an approving nod from my mother. I smiled back at her, thinking that if she knew the real reason I wanted Barrett out of the picture this afternoon, her expression would be entirely different. Crazy rage, probably.

11 :: Barrett

My first sight of the Fysher-Platt Academy didn't reassure me. Everything was on such a big scale, it made the buildings at Simplicity seem insignificant.

We were stopped at the impressive entrance by a woman in a blue uniform and lots of gold braid. She waved a small device at the barcode set into the glass in front of Aunt Kara, then motioned for us to drive through the imposing wrought iron gates. We passed under an arch that read in scintillating red letters: Fysher-Platt Academy: Premier Education Experiences Proudly Provided by Fysher Pharmaceuticals & Platt Financial Services.

Inside the gates, a collection of brooding sandstone buildings squatted in the middle of a huge expanse of grass, which was dotted with trees and clumps of flowering bushes. It was an indefensible waste of good land on which crops could have been grown. There were even several fountains spurting plumes of water into the warm air. I hoped the water was recycled, otherwise here was another heedless waste of resources.

We were driving up a wide road edged with flowerbeds. Students were wandering around in small groups, talking to each other or into Oms. Some seemed to be addressing thin air, but I'd worked out that they were using hands-free phones of some sort. No one paid attention to brightly colored carts as they zipped all over the place. Each cart had an upright panel affixed to the top on which pictures and words continually scrolled. I supposed those were advertisements, but if so, they were pointless, because nobody was looking at them.

"What are those vehicles?" I asked Taylor, who was sitting beside me in the back seat. Aunt Kara had taken over the front passenger seat with product samples she was taking to work. These included packets which, from the illustrations on them, contained some form of instant food, and many sleek metal devices, each hardly larger than a slender book.

Taylor glanced up from her green Om, where she'd been tapping out a message to someone. "What? You mean the servo-buggies? They're carrying either security guards or teachers around. Don't bother about them. All the security guards and half the teachers are nons."

She caught my puzzled expression and sighed. "You don't know anything, do you? Nons are nobodies. People you don't waste your time on, got it? There are some teachers who are okay, like Mr. Dunne, but most of them..." She shrugged.

"Teachers are nons?" This was a startling idea. At

Simplicity teaching was an honorable occupation. Anyone who taught others was always given great respect. Different people specialized in different areas of education. Uncle Paul, for example, had been responsible for teaching literature, Jane-Marie focused on physics, and Roger was the agriculture expert.

I was going to explain this to Taylor, but she'd clearly lost interest in the conversation, and was back to peering into her Om's screen. I was dutifully carrying my own Om in my pocket, but didn't expect to use it anytime soon.

When we pulled up at the largest of the sandstone buildings, Taylor gathered her things, said she'd see me later, and went off to join her friends. I followed Aunt Kara into the building. She obviously knew her way, as she strode along the wide corridor, swept past a young man behind a desk, who said, ineffectually, "Excuse me? I don't think..." and through a paneled door.

We entered a striking room, lined with many shelves loaded with leather-bound books. The furniture glowed a rich red-brown. The thick carpet was a deep burgundy.

"This is Barrett Trent, my nephew," said Aunt Kara to the woman behind the heavy, antique desk. "Barrett, Ms. Carmine-Bruett is the principal of Fysher-Platt Academy."

As we'd gotten out of the car, my aunt had reminded me not to attempt to shake hands with anyone, so I gave the principal a respectful nod.

Ms. Carmine-Bruett came out from behind the desk. She was very young, I thought, to have such a high position. She wore a tight, short, very bright pink dress that showed a good portion of her thin legs. I noticed the words Fysher-Platt Academy were woven into the material of the dress. Her jet-black hair fascinated me. It was piled on top of her head in waves and folds that seemed to defy gravity.

"Welcome to Fysher-Platt," she said, without the slightest hint of warmth in her voice. "You will be required to do a series of assessments before we can allocate you to appropriate classes."

Aunt Kara's face darkened. "I believe you've already been advised of the classes Barrett will attend."

It was Ms. Carmine-Bruett's turn to frown. "Ms. Trent, as you know, we have very strict enrolment procedures at Fysher-Platt Academy. That is how we maintain our enviable standard of excellence in the world of education."

"I spoke to Senator Rox about the matter last night. We discussed suitable classes for Barrett. The senator assured me there would be no problem."

Maynard Rox's name clearly had influence, because the principal's face immediately became smooth. "Whatever Senator Rox has decided will be quite acceptable. Barrett will be admitted to the requested classes, but will still be required to complete assessments to enable his teachers to tailor his educational programs."

Aunt Kara nodded graciously. "That's satisfactory."

The principal handed me a book-sized device, half of which was taken up by a screen. "Before you can become a student at Fysher-Platt you must agree to our non-disclo-sure policy. Please press your right thumb firmly into the indentation indicated."

Helpfully, below the screen a small red sign was blinking, *Place right thumb here.* Words appeared on the screen, and began slowly scrolling down line by line.

"You don't have to read it, Barrett," said my aunt. "It's just a formality."

"Shouldn't I know what I'm agreeing to?"

Ms. Carmine-Bruett didn't try very hard to hide her impatience. "By signing this with an electronic thumb print, you agree to the excellent provisions set up by the Fysher-Platt trustees. In essence, you are promising that you will not talk to anyone outside the school about anything at all that pertains to Fysher-Platt."

I opened my mouth to ask for further clarification, but Aunt Kara fixed me with a gimlet stare and said, "Barrett?" in such a steely tone that I pushed my thumb into the indentation without another word.

"The installation of a Safety Sentinel is mandatory," said Ms. Carmine-Bruett to my aunt.

"Of course." Aunt Kara turned to me. "You're right-handed, Barrett?"

When I nodded, she said to the principal, "The left wrist, then. Fysher-Platt's access to information from the Safety Sentinel will only apply when Barrett is on school grounds. Naturally, my access will have no restrictions."

"I'll arrange for it."

"What's a Safety Sentinel?" I asked.

Aunt Kara brushed my question aside with, "Eva will explain it to you later."

The principal summoned a small, sandy-haired man with a very thin mustache to take care of me. She addressed him by name, but I didn't catch it. Then she nodded coldly to Aunt Kara and me. "If there's anything more I can do, please don't hesitate to ask." I didn't believe she meant it.

Outside in the corridor, which was now full of people hurrying along, Aunt Kara looked at her watch and gave an irritated click of her tongue. "I've wasted too much time here already. Eva will pick you up for your dental appointment in front of this building at noon. Don't keep her waiting." Then, without even acknowledging the polite farewell from the man with the thin mustache, she left.

"I didn't get your name," I said, looking down at the much shorter man.

"Platt," he said. "Distant relative of the Platt Financial Services family." He showed his teeth in a sardonic smile. "*Very* distant."

Mr. Platt led me to a room filled with cubicles, each equipped with a desk and a chair. One was already occupied by a plump girl with a halo of frizzy brown hair, who was gazing pensively into a screen. Mr. Platt seated me in another cubicle and showed me how to operate the keyboard to answer multiple-choice questions.

"As you finish each page," he said, "press *Enter* and the next set of questions will come up on the monitor."

"Isn't this called a screen? Now you're calling it a monitor."

"It can also be called a visual display unit, or VDU."

I filed that away with the rapidly growing list of new words and concepts I was accumulating at an alarming rate. I wondered if I would ever be able to relax and take things for granted. It seemed unlikely.

Mr. Platt went to an adjoining cubicle and started tapping away on a computer with such speed that I was envious. I had to scan the keyboard for the letters and numbers I wanted, which was terribly slow.

The questions on literature I found reasonably easy, although there were some books and authors I'd never heard of before. I had no trouble with mathematics and science. Geography and history had never been my best subjects, but the questions on the screen weren't too difficult. As I suspected, there were some subjects with which I was so unfamiliar I couldn't even attempt to address the issues. I knew nothing of computing sciences, annals of advertising, consumer rights and responsibilities, and corporations and culture.

The girl finished whatever she'd been doing, and came over to talk to Mr. Platt. I heard him say, "Go back to class, Acantha. I'll call you out when your results are available."

Acantha? That was the name of the girl Taylor said had got into the second round of the *Ugly-D* competition. I craned my neck to get a good look at her, but all I caught was a view of her departing back.

At last I answered the final question and was rewarded with the words: *Thank you, Barrett Trent. This concludes assessment protocols.*

"I've finished," I said. Mr. Platt called me over to his cubicle, clicked a few buttons on his keyboard, and, with a faint whirring sound, printed sheets began to spit out of a small machine.

"Hmmm," he murmured, leafing through the pages. "Your biographical material is very sketchy—just a name and date of birth." After a much longer pause, he said, "Your results indicate you're very well informed in some areas, but know next to nothing about others."

"May I see?"

"Sorry. No student is permitted to view assessment results."

"Why not? They're *my* results, aren't they? So it follows they must belong to me."

Mr. Platt gave me an appreciative grin. "Oh, very nice argument, Barrett; however, not one to convince Fysher-Platt. All material generated by students or staff within the boundaries of the school, or created elsewhere, and intended for use in the school, automatically becomes the property of the Academy, to use any way it might choose."

This was puzzling. What possible use would my results be? "What advantage is it for the school to own everything?" I asked.

Mr. Platt glanced around, as if someone could be close

enough to overhear. This seemed an unnecessary precaution as, except for us, the room was empty. Dropping his voice to a near whisper, he said, "Lesson plans, original ideas, breakthroughs in any field taught here—all this material could conceivably generate future income for Fysher-Platt. And, quite apart from the profit motive, tight control of all information prevents anything embarrassing or damaging falling into media hands."

"Why are you whispering? Is this a secret?"

Looking rather uncomfortable, Mr. Platt said, "Of course not, but it *is* a sensitive subject." He stroked his thin mustache with one finger, as if to soothe himself, then added, "Perhaps it's better not to discuss it further."

I was intrigued. Obviously the non-disclosure agreement I'd agreed to in the principal's office had something to do with this. "What sort of information about Fysher-Platt would interest the media?"

He got to his feet, saying, "We can talk about this later. I believe your aunt said you were to be picked up at twelve? Yes? We'll have time to visit the central office, where your daily timetable will be available, together with a package of essential information given to all new students. You have your Om with you?"

I pulled it out of my pocket and showed it to him. Yesterday I'd had the choice from about ten very bright colors, and had chosen the dark red. "I'm not sure how to operate it yet."

He looked surprised, then keenly interested. "I'd heard

on the grapevine you'd had an unusual upbringing."

"I didn't find it unusual."

"So it's true you've spent most of your life without electronic communications of any sort?"

I didn't like Mr. Platt's questions, but wasn't sure why. "I haven't had to live in a noisy world, if that's what you mean."

Now he was looking thoughtful. "Have the Trents arranged for media interviews?"

"I'm not sure what you mean."

He went to say something, then made a gesture as if to dismiss the subject. "No matter." Then he paused and looked at me speculatively. "I wonder... Do you have an agent?"

Seeing my perplexity, he said, "An agent is someone who looks after your business affairs and makes sure members of the media don't take advantage of you. An agent acts as your personal representative."

I shrugged. None of this meant anything to me. When I saw her, I'd ask Taylor to explain.

"I could be your agent," said Mr. Platt in a confidential tone. "You need someone to take care of things for you."

"It doesn't seem necessary to me."

Now he was looking furtive, reminding me of a small rodent. "It would be better if you didn't mention this conversation to anyone," he said. "Anyone at all. I'll make some inquiries on your behalf, and we can take it from there."

That was the last he said on the subject, though as we walked to the central office, I was aware of him glancing sideways at me with a reflective expression.

Twenty minutes later the preliminaries of my enrolment at Fysher-Platt had been completed, ending with the insertion of a tiny device, the Safety Sentinel, under the skin of my left wrist. The white-coated man had Fysher-Platt Medical Corps written across his chest. He'd said, "This will sting a little," as he brandished an instrument that looked like an oversized hypodermic needle. It stung a lot.

Then Mr. Platt deposited me at the entrance of the main building to wait for Eva. I was early, but had much to keep me occupied. All the school information had been fed into my Om. Now all I had to do was work out what I had to do to get it to appear on the little screen...

"Senator Rox is very influential, isn't he?" I said to Eva when she picked me up in the same black vehicle we'd taken shopping yesterday.

"He certainly is that."

"Aunt Kara and the principal didn't agree about what courses I'd be doing, but when Aunt Kara mentioned Senator Rox's name, there was no further argument."

Eva paused at Fysher-Platt's front gate, then plunged our car into the stream of traffic. "Maynard Rox has been a close friend of your aunt's for many, many years. He was instrumental in setting her up as the head of the Ads-4-Life Council."

"Is he not a friend of my uncle's, too?"

She glanced over at me with a strange expression on her face. "He was once, but now, not so much."

I was puzzled by what she was saying. It seemed there was something more under the surface of her words, but I had no idea what it might be. "What do you mean?"

"Don't worry about it. I don't imagine you realize how highly regarded your uncle is. He's a world authority on the application of persuasive techniques. It's very much to Rox's advantage to have it known that Professor Adrian Stokes is one of his major supporters. It cuts both ways, of course—Rox uses his position to make sure your uncle's research is supported by government grants that allow him to remain in the forefront of his field of study."

While I was thinking this over, Eva said, "Do you understand what a politician is?"

"From my history reading, I'd define a politician as someone involved in government—a statesman or states-woman."

"Not many would call Maynard Rox a statesman, but he does have high ambitions." Eva's tone was caustic.

"What high ambitions does he have?"

"Most, if not all, politicians can visualize themselves leading the country. Maynard Rox is no different, and he has a better chance than most to achieve his goal."

I was curious, and would have asked more, but Eva changed the subject. "What did you think of the senator's son, Steve?"

"Not a great deal. And he didn't like me, either."

"That's unfortunate. At school, Steve Rox is leader of the so-called Elite Crowd."

"What's that?"

"He and his friends, including Taylor and Gabi, are the most admired group in the school population. For one thing, members have more endorsements than any other faction." Seeing my confusion, she added, "It's a form of advertising. Companies approach popular students they believe are style leaders, and pay them to use certain products that appeal to the age group."

"How could this work?" I asked, amazed. "Everyone would know they're being paid to use whatever it is."

"Companies wouldn't employ the technique if it didn't increase sales," said Eva. "Kids see someone popular using a particular brand name, and they want to imitate the person."

"Do these style leaders have agents?"

Eva raised her eyebrows. "Agents? Where did you hear that term?"

I told her about Mr. Platt's offer to be my agent. Her expression grew grim. "Don't agree to anything."

"I haven't."

"I'll speak to your aunt. Mr. Platt won't be worrying you again."

"He asked me not to tell anyone. I don't want to get him into trouble."

Eva gave a derisive snort. "The man abused his position

by trying to take advantage of you, Barrett. That's unfor-givable."

She switched to my appointment with the dentist, explaining how Dr. Selkirk's offices had a wonderful view of the surrounding city because they were near the top of a skyscraper.

The highest I'd ever been was the summit of the hills near Simplicity. While I was thinking what it must be like to be higher than the birds, Eva jolted me with, "Have you had an anesthetic before?"

"No, never. Why would I need an anesthetic?"

"Your aunt seems to think you may require extensive dental work."

I felt a wave of irritation. Aunt Kara appeared to be adept at jumping to conclusions about me. "How could she think that? I've never had any trouble with my teeth."

"If that's so, you don't have to worry about an anesthetic," Eva said as she steered the car into a parking area underneath a building that went up and up into the sky. "You'll be in and out of Dr. Selkirk's dental chair in just a few minutes."

That didn't happen.

First, Dr. Selkirk directed his assistant, a wispy woman with an expressionless face, to take X-rays of my mouth. X-rays! All I knew about Madame Curie and the way she and her husband had died from radiation rushed into my mind. "I'd rather not have an X-ray."

"Why ever not?"

I explained about radiation. Dr. Selkirk patted my shoulder. "There's nothing to worry about. Your exposure will be minuscule."

Eva was brought in from the waiting room to persuade me. With trepidation, I agreed to have my teeth irradiated.

"Hmmm," said Dr. Selkirk, peering at the ghostly shadow of my jaw displayed on a screen. "Hmmm." He turned to me. "Well, son, you have pain in this lower back molar." He indicated the right side of my face.

"No, never."

"The decay hasn't reached the nerve yet. But it will. Very soon." His own teeth were extremely white when he flashed them in a smile. "You've come to me just in time. I wouldn't want you to endure, even for a moment, the agony of an abscessed tooth. We can't have that." He gestured to his assistant to ready herself. "Happily, we can do something about your problem this afternoon."

Dr. Selkirk was nothing like gruff old Dr. Browne, who did the checkups at Simplicity. Dr. Selkirk's artificial friendliness put me on my guard. I was about to say I'd rather delay the treatment when the dental chair in which I was seated suddenly tilted, so I was lying back, at Dr. Selkirk's mercy.

"I don't want any type of anesthetic," I said.

"It's normal to be nervous," he said breezily. "Just leave everything to me."

Twisting my head, I could see he was holding something

in one hand. Before I could protest, I heard a hiss and felt a faint stinging sensation on the skin of my forearm. Then the edges of everything began to blur, to dissolve into darkness. The last thing I saw was Dr. Selkirk's very white teeth, displayed in a cheerful smile.

12 :: Taylor

I could hardly hear Gabi above the music. It was always noisy at Ruby & Jake's, but today Melted Organs' *Retro Heavy Metal* was on the video wall, and the sound blasting out was loud enough to hurt.

"Come downstairs!" she yelled. "Fergus has something he says is the best yet. Delia and Hart are game to try it. I said I wouldn't. No way."

Fergus always had the latest party drug. Got them through his dad, he said, which could well be true. His father was an executive in Fysher Pharmaceuticals, and the company had the government contract to analyze new designer drugs when they turned up on the party circuit.

I looked around. "Have you seen Steve? I saw him at lunch today and we made a date to meet here after school."

"A date?" said Gabi, grinning. "That's progress." She grabbed my arm. "You don't want to look as if you're hanging around waiting for him. Let Steve go to the trouble of finding you."

"Where's Nat?" I asked as we clattered down the stairs to the basement. "You said he was coming with you today."

She made a face. "He's finishing some dumb science experiment. Something to do with Q-Plague. He might be along later."

Nat hardly ever came to the cyberparlor, and when he did, it was obvious he hated being there.

"You haven't got anything in common," I said, for the fortieth time.

Gabi shrugged. Topic closed.

I was wasting my breath telling her it would never work, but I knew I was totally right. Nat was way too serious for Gabi, and he didn't fit in with our crowd.

It was much quieter in the basement, even though it was full of people playing the old arcade machines, which were set up in rows. There was a curtained alcove in the farthest corner where our group usually met up. Fergus, Delia, and Hart were already there. Hart was slumped in a chair playing with his Om, Delia was standing by Fergus, looking doubtfully at the tiny pink pills in the palm of his hand.

"Oh, come on, Delia," Fergus was saying. "Juff's absolutely a blast. You'll love what it does for you. And I'll give you a good price."

"I'm not sure..."

"Don't do it, Delia," said Gabi. "Didn't you hear about that girl at the party last week who took juffs and then had convulsions and died? They rushed her to hospital, but the doctors couldn't save her."

"*What* girl?" said Fergus scornfully. "It's a cybertale, Gabi. You'd believe anything."

Gabi raised her eyebrows. "Like you'd know."

"I heard it wasn't juffs that killed her," said Hart, glancing up from his Om. "It was Q-Plague."

We all looked at him. I shivered. The plagues in general, and Q-Plague in particular, were terrifying. Millions had died in poor countries, but I'd only heard of a couple of cases here, and the disease hadn't spread. The thing was, though, Q-Plague killed almost everyone who caught it.

"You're kidding, right?" said Fergus.

Hart raised his shoulders. "I'm only repeating what I heard."

"It wasn't on the news," said Gabi.

"They're keeping it quiet. People panic."

"You're full of it, Hart," said Fergus. "My dad would know if there was an outbreak, and he hasn't said anything."

"What's going on?"

It was Steve. My heart gave a jump. He was *so* cool, and had the cutest dimple right in the middle of his chin.

"So where's your farmie cousin?" Steve asked me. "Aren't you supposed to be holding his hand?"

"Yeah," said Delia. "Where is he? We've all heard about him." She grinned at me. "Can he speak English, or does he just point and grunt?"

Hart snapped his Om closed, dropped into a crouch and mimed a caveman, scratching his chest and then making wild gestures while grunting loudly. Everyone laughed.

I laughed too, but felt bad about it. "Barrett had to go to the dentist," I said.

Delia then made a rude comment about country nons and rotten teeth, and I surprised myself with how annoyed I felt. After all, he *was* my cousin, and it wasn't fair to make fun of him when he wasn't there to defend himself.

Before I could decide if I should say something, Fergus snapped, "Look, Delia, do you want to try juffs, or not? I'm wasting time here."

"Will it pass a Chemscan?"

"Sure, sure." Fergus was getting more and more impatient. "What about you, Hart? Got the dollars?"

Hart shook his head. "I can pay you next week."

"No pay, no way."

"I've got purple jolters," said Steve.

"Jolters?" Fergus practically sneered. "Soft stuff."

"I can guarantee a Chemscan won't pick them up."

Delia gave Steve a big smile. "Okay, Steve. How much?"

"One capsule. Free. This time."

Delia gave Steve a sexy smile, and put a hand on his arm. Ugh!

"I'll try a purple, Steve," I said quickly.

Steve fished a box out of his pocket and put a capsule in the center of my palm. "Only one's free, and it's first in, first served."

Delia stuck out her bottom lip. "What about me?"

I tried to hide my amusement when Steve said mockingly, "What about you?"

Delia gave us both a nasty look and walked off. She was heading for Nessa Young, her best friend. Bad news! Being on the wrong side of Delia was bad enough, but Nessa was queen bee, and had the meanest mouth in the school.

She wouldn't say anything about Steve—he was too popular—but she'd never liked me much, so I was fair game. Dire! Everyone listened to her. I made a note to look for them both later, and find some way to smooth things over.

I examined the purple capsule in my hand. All the cybertales weren't made up. People did sometimes get sick, and even die. But I worried more about the stories about kids who'd fried the wiring in their brains, so they'd never be the same again. Gabi, arms folded, was watching me. I said to her, "What do you think?"

Steve frowned at me. "What's your problem? I thought you'd be game to try anything, Taylor. Maybe I was wrong."

The lights dimmed, then brightened, then dimmed again. We all stopped and stared at the panels in the ceiling. The sequence was repeated.

"Shit!" said Steve. "It's a raid!"

13 :: Barrett

As soon as I got into the car, I said to Eva, "I told Dr. Selkirk I didn't want an anesthetic, but he ignored me and gave me one anyway. That's not right!"

"I understand your aunt had given her permission for the procedure."

Now I was really angry. "I don't have any say at all about what happens to me?"

I expected her to say something soothing, but instead Eva said in a dry tone, "Apparently not."

I was still a bit lightheaded from the anesthetic and my jaw was aching, so when we reached the house and Eva suggested I lie down, I went along with the idea. I even dozed off for a while, but woke up feeling hungry, which wasn't surprising, as I hadn't had anything to eat since breakfast.

On my way to the kitchen, I heard raised voices, loud enough to drown out the ambient music that was always playing in the house.

I slowed to a stop in the hallway. I'd never heard Aunt

Kara yell before, and found it decidedly intimidating.

"I have to congratulate you, Taylor! You've really done it this time!"

"I didn't *do* anything."

"My daughter suspected of selling drugs! The media will have a field day. Your father will be furious, but not as angry as I am right now."

"I'm trying to tell you, Mom. Nessa and Delia told the cops I was selling juffs. It wasn't true."

Aunt Kara raged on. "How could you do this? Be caught trading illegal drugs like some feral kid on the streets?"

"I wasn't!"

"Then tell me who was."

"No one. It was all a mistake."

"You're grounded."

"But, Mom—"

"Don't argue with me, Taylor. And as for the matter of the GPS displacer..."

Fascinated, but feeling guilty about eavesdropping, I hurried along to the kitchen, where Eva was making preparations for the evening meal.

"Aunt Kara's yelling at Taylor," I said.

"That young woman's got herself into hot water, and not for the first time."

"My aunt said Taylor was grounded. What does that mean?"

"She gets to stay home. I imagine Taylor is about to lose all her privileges, including seeing any of her friends.

And she won't be attending classes. Fysher-Platt has very strict rules about drugs. Even the suggestion that Taylor had anything to do with something illegal is enough to bar her from school until this is resolved."

"I overheard Aunt Kara mentioning a GPS displacer. What is that?"

"Do you know what the global positioning system is?"

"I think so." We had studied artificial satellites and their uses in physics classes. "Signals are bounced off satellites to establish the exact point where you are on the ground. That's it, isn't it?"

"Exactly. You've been chipped, haven't you?"

I rubbed my wrist, which was still tender. "Do you mean the Safety Sentinel? I got one earlier today."

"The Safety Sentinel is one of the most popular products of the Locatomatic Corporation. It's heavily advertised to parents as a security device that will bring peace of mind because the chip sends a continuous GPS signal that can establish exactly where a child is at any given moment."

"And a GPS displacer sends a false position?"

Eva nodded. "Sharp of you, Barrett. That's exactly what it does. I'm not surprised Taylor's been using a displacer—she's a techno-savvy kid—but I am surprised that up to this point she's concealed it from her parents so effectively, considering how closely she's monitored."

Every question I asked generated another question, and then another. "What do you mean, Taylor's closely monitored?"

Eva looked away. "It's not important," she said quickly. "You must be hungry, Barrett. I'll get you a snack. Don't eat too much, though, you'll ruin your dinner."

::

"I suppose you've heard." Taylor looked angry and upset and rebellious, all at once.

I'd run into my cousin on the stairs on my way back from the kitchen. "Do you want to talk about it?" I asked.

She shrugged. "What's there to say? It doesn't matter how much I try to explain, no one listens."

"I'll listen."

"Yeah, thanks," she said dismissively. She shot out her lower lip. "Mom's even taken my Om. And no games, no TV, no nothing. And now she's sent me to my room like a little kid, until Dad comes home."

Shoulders slumped, hands rammed into the pockets of her jeans, she mounted the last steps to the upper hallway. Her bedroom was first on the right. She shoved open the door with her shoulder and clomped inside.

"You might as well come in," she called out. "I've got nothing better to do."

"Such a gracious invitation," I said. "How could I resist?"

That got a small smile. Then she sighed. "You've no clue how totally dire this all is for me."

I'd left the door open. It didn't seem right to be in my cousin's bedroom with it shut. I looked around and found a chair. The colors here were warm ones—pale rose shading to the dusky red of the thick carpet.

There was music playing; an insistent beat as maddeningly even as a metronome. Taylor must have read something in my expression, because she said, "Want it off?"

"Yes, please."

She punched a button on her desk. The beat stopped.

"I'm accustomed to silence," I said.

Tilting her head, Taylor regarded me closely. "I guess you feel like you've been dropped onto another planet."

"Something like that. Now tell me what happened today."

I was rather surprised when she did, quite freely. She didn't even seem to mind when I asked questions about what made one drug illegal and another not.

"So the police officers didn't find any incriminating evidence on you?" I said.

Taylor shook her head. "Everyone with anything dumped whatever they had before the cops could get downstairs."

"So it's just the word of these two people, Delia and Nessa, that you were selling drugs. That's it? Nothing else?"

"Nessa's mother is high up in the police," said Taylor bitterly, "so who do you think they're going to believe?"

"I'd believe you," I said.

"Well, thanks, Barrett, that's a big help." She let out her breath in another big sigh.

We sat silently for a moment, then I said, "Can I ask you something?"

"What?"

"When I arrived on Saturday, Eva asked if my room should be quiescent or activated. Your mother said quiescent. What did she mean?"

My question quite cheered Taylor up. "Come with me," she said, making for the door. "You have to see it to believe it."

"Shouldn't you be staying in your room?"

Taylor gave me a look of deep pity. "Honestly! You're such a goody-goody, cousin. Do you always play by the rules?"

"If the reason behind the rule is worthy, yes."

She shook her head. "Unbelievable."

I followed her down the hallway to my bedroom. She marched into the walk-in wardrobe, which was now more respectable. It was one-third filled with the clothes and shoes Eva had bought for me yesterday.

"See this?" said Taylor, opening a small box on the wall that I hadn't noticed before. Inside was a switch with a light beside it glowing red. "Let's turn it on." The light changed to green.

She led the way out into my room. "Dad had this suite wired up as an experiment in persuasion. It's got all the latest stuff. Try it. Go into the bathroom."

As soon as I stepped through the bathroom door, a warm voice said, "Irregular? Kolonic Komfort brings welcome relief." As the words were spoken, *Kolonic Komfort* appeared at the top of the mirror over the wash-basin. The voice continued, "Try our free sample, and say to yourself, 'There's no relief like Kolonic Komfort relief!'"

"A different ad will play each time you come through the door," Taylor said. "Look in the cupboard under the basin. There should be product samples."

I opened the cupboard to find she was right. Apart from Kolonic Komfort, I found shampoo, face cream, mouthwash, and toothpaste.

"That's not all," said Taylor, clearly enjoying my bemused expression. "Once the system is activated, your pillow will talk to you all night long. The moment its sensors feel the weight of your head, it starts off with lullabies. Then, when it detects you're asleep, soft little voices will start planting ideas about products you should buy."

"Subliminal suggestions. Uncle Paul taught me it was an insidious way to get through to the unconscious mind."

"Watch this next bit," said Taylor, making for my bed. "This is really good." She seized my pillow. "Let's say you can't stand being talked to, so you get rid of it."

She tossed the pillow on the floor. Immediately an urgent voice began chanting, "Pick me up! Pick me up!"

Laughing, she snatched the pillow from the floor and replaced it on my bed. The voice fell silent.

"I can't imagine how anyone would be willing to endure all this," I said. "It's just so annoying."

"You'd be surprised," said Taylor. "Let's say a guy's

staying in a hotel. He gets a credit for every ad that plays while he's in the room. When he leaves, he can cash in the credits for a prize, or use them to buy tickets in a lottery that's drawn every week."

I had the uncomfortable thought that maybe the intention had been to wait until I'd settled in, and then to activate the system without warning me about it. "Are any other rooms in the house set up like this?"

Taylor shook her head. "Just this one." She grinned. "There are other bedrooms you could have been given, but I think Mom was going to run a little experiment on you. Now I've just blown it by showing you how to turn the system off."

A sudden spurt of anger made me say, "What gives your mother the right to experiment on me?"

"Taylor, where are you?"

"Jeez," said Taylor, hearing her father's voice. She ran for the door. "I've had it now."

14 :: Barrett

Uncle Adrian frowned at Taylor across the breakfast table. "It's hardly fair to Barrett," he said. "Thanks to your little escapade, he'll have to attend classes without your help."

There were three of us at the table: my uncle, Taylor, and me. Aunt Kara had already left for an early appointment, which was fortunate—if she'd been there, Taylor would still be banished to her bedroom.

"The person it's not fair to is *me*." Taylor's face was mutinous. "I've been blamed for something I didn't do. I've told you a thousand times I wasn't selling drugs, but you and Mom don't believe me."

"Drugs were found at the cyberparlor, and I'd say it's likely, given his past record, that Fergus Fysher was involved. And he belongs to your group of friends."

"Guilt by association," I said.

My uncle shot me a surprised look. "You're defending Taylor?"

"I'm just saying that 'Birds of a feather flock together' isn't the same as hard evidence."

With an unwilling smile, he conceded, "That's true." His smile disappeared as he turned back to my cousin. "The fact remains you deceived your mother, and you deceived me. You deliberately negated your Safety Sentinel with a GPS displacer to show you were somewhere other than Ruby & Jake's Cyberparlor. That was dishonest and devious."

"Everyone does it."

"That's not an adequate defense. How long have you been using a displacer?"

Taylor looked uncomfortable. "Awhile."

"I'd appreciate something more definite," he said coldly.

"A few months."

"So you've been dishonest for a few months?"

Taylor shrugged, mumbling something about being sorry.

Her father glared at her. "What did you say?"

"I said I'm sorry. Really sorry." She looked imploringly at him. "Dad, do I have to be grounded? I mean, Barrett needs me."

That got a bark of laughter from Uncle Adrian. "Oh, *please,*" he said. "Don't use your cousin as your get-out-of-jail card. You know very well that Fysher-Platt won't let you through the gate until your name's cleared. Your mother's with Senator Rox now, trying to find a way out of this mess."

For the first time, Taylor looked hopeful. "Uncle

Maynard can fix it for me—he knows everybody."

"Excuse me," said Eva from the doorway, "but Barrett has to leave in ten minutes if he's to be on time for school."

I gulped down the last of my toast and orange juice, said a hasty goodbye to Uncle Adrian and Taylor, and rushed up to my room to clean my teeth, being careful with my back molar, which was still tender. When I came down the stairs, Eva was waiting for me at the front door.

"Have you got your Om?" she asked as we walked to the garage.

"Yes, but I still don't really know how to use it. I think I can find my class timetable, but that's about all."

"I'll run through its functions with you this afternoon." She passed me a thin metal bracelet. "Put this on, it's an identity bracelet. It can also be used to carry out financial transactions. You can use your Om to pay for items, but in the meantime, this is a simpler method. It will automatically debit your account when you purchase something, for example, when you have lunch today."

"Aunt Kara mentioned giving me an allowance, but I don't believe I have an account to debit."

"You do, now. Your aunt has set it up for you."

I was silent on the drive to Fysher-Platt Academy. I wasn't happy that Aunt Kara and Uncle Adrian were providing me not only with a roof over my head, but with money, when I had no way at all of paying it back. Perhaps there was something I could do to earn what I'd be spending. I looked down at the unfamiliar dark jacket and pants I was wearing, and the shoes, so much lighter than boots. The clothing Eva had bought for me must have cost a lot. I would have to find out how much, so I could keep a running total of what I owed. Aunt Kara had told me not to worry about it, but I was determined to repay every dollar.

My attention was caught by a news strip running along the front of an office building. I'd glanced at it yesterday, but had been too anxious about Fysher-Platt to pay much attention. Today, because the traffic was stopped right next to it, I had time to examine the strip closely.

Safe & Sound Security brings you breaking news on latest terrorist outrage... Remember, Three S's means You & Your Loved Ones are Safe! This was followed by details of a suicide bombing. A vitamin company sponsored the next news item, which covered a study showing how many people's diets failed to include enough essential minerals and vitamins.

"Can companies choose the news they sponsor?" I asked Eva.

"Of course. The advertising message is much more effective if it's tied to something real. Companies pay a premium to be linked to breaking news stories."

"But there must be some news with which a business wouldn't want to be associated."

Eva's smile was cynical. "I can't think of any. No

matter how distasteful or violent a story, there's always an angle."

When we reached the school, Eva reminded me that we were going shopping again this afternoon for items Fysher-Platt Academy required each student to have. These included sports equipment and clothes, and an electronic book reader.

I waved goodbye to her and went straight to the central office, as I'd been told to do yesterday when I received my timetable. The same cheerful woman smiled at me. "Barrett Trent! Back again, so soon?"

"Yes, ma'am."

She chuckled. "Ma'am, is it? I love you polite country boys. Now let's see..." She tapped her keyboard, staring into a screen. "Yes, here it is. You'll be paired for today with another student who's only been at Fysher-Platt for a few months, and remembers what it's like to be new at the school. She'll be able to show you around and familiarize you with the Academy. Her name is Acantha Brown. You'll find her in"—more tapping of keys—"Room Eighteen of Block Five. Science will be your first class of the day."

Armed with directions and a site map, thankfully on a sheet of paper, and not on the screen of my Om, I set off for Block Five. Acantha was such an unusual name, I was sure it was the same girl I'd seen when I'd been evaluated yesterday, the person Taylor had talked about as being a contestant on the *Ugly-D to Teen Queen* program.

Like the day before, there were students wandering all

over the grounds, most of them using their Oms. I stood out in some way—perhaps my red hair and freckles—because several of them noticed me and said something to their companions. A few said "Hi," which seemed to be the accepted way of greeting people. And two smiled at me, which made me feel a little more welcome.

When a siren sounded, everyone was galvanized into action. Obviously the siren was an indication that lessons were about to begin, so like everyone else, I picked up speed. Reaching Block Five, I joined a mass of students in the corridors. Room Eighteen was rapidly filling. I hesitated at the doorway, looking for Acantha Brown. There she was, near the back. It was a help I'd caught a glimpse of her before, otherwise I would have had to ask someone to point her out to me.

"Acantha?" I said, looming over her. She was rather plump, and had frizzy hair, but I couldn't see why she thought she might need a total makeover to transform her into somebody else when she was a perfectly pleasant-looking person.

"You're Barrett Trent? I've saved a seat for you."

"Hello," I said. "I saw you yesterday, when I was with Mr. Platt."

I slid into the desk beside her. It had a glowing screen set into its surface. Along the top edge of the screen were the words: *Your desk is underwritten by Begone! Pain Relief.*

I looked around. Almost every place was taken, and the

room was filled with the buzz of conversation. I became aware that people were looking at me with open curiosity, which made me feel as if I were on display.

"You have to identify yourself." Acantha showed me how to wave my bracelet over the screen. It gave a soft burp, then *Welcome, Barrett Trent* appeared. Then the words: *Reminder: no student may use a personal electronic device in class.*

"The teacher has a master screen," Acantha said. "Each desk shows details of the person sitting there. Results, reports—everything can be called up."

"There won't be anything on me, yet," I said.

Acantha was amused. "When you enrolled yesterday, you did a set of assessment tests. All those results, plus a full background search, will already be in the central data bank."

It was somehow appalling to realize strangers had access to all this information about me. "I can understand why the test results are useful," I said, "but what's the background search for?"

Acantha seemed surprised I'd asked. "To tailor advertising to meet your personal needs."

I couldn't see what personal needs I had that advertising could meet, but before I could comment on this, a hush fell as the teacher came into the room. He was a brawny man with very little neck, and as he walked to the front podium he was putting on a loose top over the shirt he was already wearing. It proclaimed: *This science period is brought to you by Blissjoy Mood Lighteners—"Make Life Shine Again!"*

When a siren signaled the end of the period, which had been fairly basic physics, the teacher actually said, "And remember, students, this science period has been brought to you by Blissjoy Mood Lighteners. Don't be blue, don't be sad. Blissjoy Mood Lighteners will make your life shine again."

"We have corporations and culture next," said Acantha, standing up. She was taller than I'd realized. "It's not what you'd call my best subject. That's why I was there yesterday, when you saw me. I had to do a remedial test because I bombed the one in class."

"You must be Barrett! I'm Gabi, Taylor's best friend in the whole world." Suddenly a blue-eyed blonde girl was smiling at me.

"Hello," I said.

"I can see why she didn't send me a pic. You're *so* good-looking."

"I beg your pardon?"

"I totally begged Taylor to zap a pic of you, but she didn't. Keeping you to herself, I guess."

I had to smile, thinking of how Taylor had made it clear she would rather I wasn't there at all. "Somehow I doubt that."

"We'll be late for class," said Acantha.

"Oh, hi, Acantha," said Gabi. "How'd you score this guy?"

"I was asked to show him around, that's all."

Gabi winked at me. "Hey, if you want a change, I'm available."

Seeing Acantha's unhappy, resigned expression, I said quickly, "Thank you, but I'll stay with Acantha."

As Acantha and I walked to our next class in Block Three, she said to me, "Gabi's one of the most popular girls in the whole school. If you want her to show you around instead of me, the central office could probably arrange it."

"I don't want a change... unless you're trying to get rid of me."

"I'm not."

"So let's leave it as it is."

My desk in the corporations and culture classroom was sponsored by Ubiquitous Communications, and the period itself was brought to students by Platt Financial Services.

I had no idea what corporations and culture might be as a subject, but soon found it was close to Uncle Paul's definition of propaganda. The case study we were doing today related to the surveillance industry.

The teacher, Ms. Ives, was a small woman with a high voice and emphatic gestures. Her first words from the podium at the front of the room were directed at Acantha, who was sitting at the desk beside me. "Acantha, this is simply not good enough! You barely passed your remedial test. It seems you entirely fail to appreciate the priceless contributions corporations make to enrich our culture. I will not have you fail this course! You will have additional homework until further notice."

I glanced over at Acantha, who was rolling her eyes. Someone behind us hissed, "Freakoid." I didn't think he meant the teacher.

Ms. Ives didn't stay long at the podium. Soon she was bouncing around the classroom in an excess of energy, now and then punching the air with an upraised fist when she made a particularly important point.

When near my desk, she had one of these air-punching moments. "The demand for personal privacy!" she exclaimed. "What is it? Let me answer that!" She punched the air. "The demand for personal privacy is a selfish, self-centered desire to exclude oneself from the very fabric of our society!"

Perhaps my expression showed the doubt I felt about the right of surveillance companies to know everything about everybody, because Ms. Ives fixed me with a belligerent stare. "Yes?" she said, "Do you have something to say?"

There was a stir in the class. I heard someone whisper, "It's Taylor Trent's farmie cousin."

"I can't see what's wrong with wanting some measure of privacy," I said.

"Ah!" She seized on my comment with obvious delight. "What's wrong with the individual demanding privacy? Can someone answer that?"

"Our society thrives on information," said a dark girl

with blood-red fingernails so long I wondered how she could operate the tiny buttons on her Om. "To deny corporations information is to deny them the lifeblood that invigorates our culture."

This sounded so much like something she was parroting from a textbook, I looked at Ms. Ives with the expectation that she would criticize this comment as being facile and unfounded.

I found the teacher punching the air again. "Yes! Campbell is absolutely right. The wellsprings of our culture spring from the rich torrent of data that pours into our corporations every day. Without that enrichment, our society would stagnate."

I shook my head. Surely everyone in the room couldn't believe this? Was I the only one with doubts? I caught Acantha looking at me. There was sympathy on her face. "You'll learn to fake it," she said. "It's the easiest way."

"You don't seem to be taking your own advice."

She gave me a sour smile. "I don't, do I?"

15 :: Barrett

My class before lunch was English. Acantha led the way, plunging into the river of chattering students—most talking on their Oms—heading for Block Two. When I caught up to her, she said, "Our English teacher is Mr. Dunne. You'll find him rather iconoclastic."

I looked at Acantha with new respect, having so far not heard a word like this from anyone at Fysher-Platt Academy. "How so?"

"I'm afraid Mr. Dunne doesn't have a high regard for the cherished beliefs of our school," she said with a mocking smile.

Steve Rox was sauntering into the classroom when Acantha and I arrived with a knot of other students. He paused, looked me up and down, then sniffed the air elaborately. "I think I smell fertilizer," he said with a sneer. "There must be some dumb farmie around."

His companion, a skinny boy I hadn't seen before, laughed.

I would have completely ignored Steve Rox, if Acantha

hadn't observed, "It must be because you're full of it, Rox."

This time several people laughed. Steve Rox reddened, plainly astonished at her audacity. "Ugly bitch," he ground out. "You need some manners slapped into you."

I grabbed his wrist as he raised his arm to strike her. "Apologize," I said.

Struggling to free himself, he snarled, "Why? She *is* an ugly bitch who needs to be taught a lesson."

I was used to hard physical labor; he was not. And I had the advantage of learning wrestling from Gordon, who'd been an Olympian before joining Simplicity.

I tightened my grip, and with one quick move, had him down on his knees, his arm behind his back. "Apologize to Acantha, please."

"Wow!" said somebody. I looked up to find we were surrounded by a growing crowd. There was a murmur of appreciation. I wondered if perhaps Steve was not much liked.

"Let me go," he growled, vainly trying to free himself.

"Of course. When you apologize."

"To her?" He sent Acantha a venomous look. "She's nothing but a—"

He cried out as I shoved his arm farther up his back. "Apologize."

"Jesus! Okay, I'm sorry," he spat out. "Now let me go."

As I helped him to his feet, Acantha said to me, "The teacher's here. Play it cool."

"What exactly is going on here?" Mr. Dunne was a soft-spoken man, balding and running to fat, but he had a sharply intelligent face.

"Nothing," said Steve Rox, his face swollen with suppressed rage. "Absolutely nothing."

"Then everybody to their desks, and we'll start."

As he pushed past me, Steve Rox hissed, "You're finished, Trent. Dead and gone. Count on it."

"Mr. Dunne?" said Acantha. "This is Barrett Trent. He's starting classes today."

"Ah, yes," said Mr. Dunne, "I've met your uncle. I took a very interesting seminar from Professor Adrian Stokes last year on the latest developments in the use of persuasive psychology in politics. Welcome to the class, Barrett."

I found a seat next to Acantha. My heart was still hammering hard after my confrontation with Steve Rox, but I was sure my face didn't show my anger and disgust.

My desk informed me that it had been sponsored by the antiviral Cue-Kill, lately developed by Fysher Pharmaceuticals to combat Q-Plague.

"Cute, isn't it?" Acantha said, leaning over to look at my screen. "Cue-Kill kills Q-Plague."

I glanced around to see where Steve Rox was sitting. He was two rows across from me. He caught me looking at him and glowered in my direction. He hadn't liked me much before. Now, because I had shamed him in front of everyone, I guessed he hated me.

At the front of the room, Mr. Dunne was removing his advertising overshirt, which announced the English class today was brought to us by *Famous Flidder! You deserve the best! Flidder, the creamy ice cream countless taste buds crave in 69 fantastic Flidder flavors!*

He draped the overshirt on a chair, so the wording was clearly visible. His voice came from a speaker in my desk. "Today we examine the techniques of persuasion, using as our first example, Famous Flidder Ice Cream." There was a note of scorn in his voice when he said the brand name.

"Persuasion in advertising frequently uses many of the strategies employed by propaganda and political campaigns," he went on. "These strategies include repeating the same message over and over with strong conviction, as if by doing this it somehow makes the message true, deliberate exaggeration, unsubstantiated claims, and appeals to the audience's emotions, not their intellects."

On my screen, a series of advertisements for Flidder Ice Cream appeared, running one after the other. They were very alike, being loud, repetitious, and filled with joyous ice cream eaters.

"The Flidder Company claims independent assessment proves it is the premier ice cream. But is this true? Apparently not. Blindfold taste tests have this brand very near the bottom of the list of preferred ice creams."

In my screen a summary page from an industry report appeared, with the description of Flidder Ice

Cream highlighted as "unpleasant, chalky texture with pronounced chemical aftertaste."

"There's going to be trouble," said Acantha. "Flidder is a Fysher-Platt–accredited sponsor. The company supplies the school restaurant. It's forbidden to criticize a sponsor, even as a joke."

"I don't think Mr. Dunne is joking," I said.

"Does Flidder Ice Cream come in sixty-nine flavors?" Mr. Dunne inquired. "Again, no. An investigation by Fair Play in the Marketplace, an independent consumer organization, found only twenty-two separate flavors. To bring the total to sixty-nine, many of these flavors had more than one name. For example, Blackcurrant Burst was also marketed as Berry Beautiful."

He paused, then added, "Would it surprise you to learn that Fair Play is being sued by Flidder for maliciously destroying the company's corporate reputation? This is a technique of intimidation, used by many organizations to stifle legitimate consumer criticism."

"Someone will report him for this," Acantha said dolefully.

Glancing over at Steve Rox, I saw that, against the rules, he had his Om out, and was tapping a message into it.

"I think someone already has," I said.

::

When Eva picked me up after school, she drove to the same huge shopping complex we'd gone to on Sunday.

Our plunge into the underground parking at Shoppaganza no longer alarmed me. Every day I added a paragraph or more to a letter I was writing to my friends at Simplicity, and I realized I'd have to start explaining how quickly things at first completely strange to me had become almost familiar.

Eva parked, and we walked through to the shopping area. The complex was just as packed with people as before, advertisements still flashed and scintillated, music blasted out at a deafening volume, warring smells of food and perfumes filled the air. I could become accustomed to many things in the Chattering World, I thought, but not this sustained assault on my senses.

We were just about to enter a sporting goods store when suddenly silence fell. The shriek of advertising died as all the screens went blank.

It wasn't completely silent, though—there was still the murmur of voices, as people looked around, puzzled.

"It can't be a power failure," I said to Eva, "because the lights are still on."

With a trace of grim satisfaction in her voice, she said, "It's ADA."

Eva spoke with such conviction that I stared at her. "Who's Ada?" I asked, "and why is she doing this?"

"It's not a person," Eva said. "The initials ADA stand for Against Deceit in Advertising. ADA's an underground protest group. They temporarily sabotage the advertising system in large venues like this so they can run anti-ads.

Watch the screens. They'll start in a moment."

As if on her command, the screens sprang back to life, each showing the same image. A flock of cartoon sheep stood looking out with dim expressions on their long faces. Every now and then one said, "Baaa." The initials ADA appeared in red letters above their heads.

"Don't be consumer sheep," warned a deep, command-ing voice. "Think for yourself. Don't allow yourself to be herded into conformity."

The images on the screens changed to a cartoon man, his limbs tied in knots around his body. As he rolled around, trying to untangle himself, the voice said, "This is brought to you as a public service by Against Deceit in Advertising. Don't allow yourself to be manipulated and your thoughts controlled. Don't believe everything you're told. Be warned: most advertisements lie, twist the truth, deceive. Be skeptical. Ask who benefits. Do you? Or is your hard-earned money lining the pockets of greedy multinational corporations?"

A squad of security guards in dark gray uniforms came pushing through the crowd. One of them raised something to his mouth, and his amplified voice boomed out. "Report anyone suspicious to the nearest guard. Substan-tial rewards are paid immediately for useful information. Check out everyone close to you. Members of ADA are traitors to our economy."

I asked Eva, "Are these guards the same as police officers?"

"Not at all. They're private security, hired by the shopping complex." She added with a grim expression, "That doesn't stop most of them behaving as if they have all the authority in the world."

"So they can't arrest anyone?"

"They can hold a suspect until the police arrive, that's all."

I looked at one of the gray-uniformed men. He had a truncheon in one hand, and the other was clamped on the butt of his holstered firearm. "The guards are armed," I said. "Do they shoot people?"

Eva's mouth tightened. "I'm afraid they do. Far too often." She added with a sardonic smile, "But always with a good excuse."

Above our heads, the screens changed again. With astonishment I saw my Aunt Kara's likeness. Behind her the Ads-4-Life name appeared with its motto: *Improving your world every day.*

"The Ads-4-Life Council," boomed out the same resonant voice that had been on the two previous anti-ads, "does *not* improve *your* world. It improves the *corporate* world. The Council is a propaganda machine, spewing out misinformation and half truths."

The face of another person I recognized flashed onto the screens—Senator Maynard Rox. There was a slogan above his head: *Maynard Rox cares! He supports you! Support him!*

As a red line was drawn through these words, the

voice intoned, "Maynard Rox does not care for citizens like you, he cares for the welfare of his corporate masters. Ask yourself who *really* supports Maynard Rox."

After a short pause, the speaker continued, "Fysher Pharmaceuticals have secretly bankrolled Rox's campaign with millions of dollars. Ask yourself *why*. What does all this money buy? Silence. It buys silence. Silence about the Q-Plague that has escaped from Fysher's research laboratories, and is spreading through our population without a single alarm bell being sounded."

A ripple ran through the mass of people. "Q-Plague? What did he say about Q-Plague?"

The screens flickered, went blank, and came up again with Senator Rox's image, then blanked for a final time.

Some distance from us there was a commotion. Many people rushed to get out of the way, others put up their arms, holding something in their hands.

"What are they doing?" I asked Eva.

"Using their Oms to take video or photos to send to their friends if it turns out to be something interesting. Sometimes people make a lot of money selling a particularly spectacular shot to the media."

I craned my neck to see what was happening. Several security guards were holding a violently struggling man.

Beside me Eva said, "Oh, no."

"They've got someone from ADA," came from the crowd.

Eva's thin face was gaunt. "Let's get out of here," she

said to me. "We'll finish your shopping another day."

"Do you know him? The man the guards have?"

"No," she said sharply. "Of course I don't."

I didn't believe her.

16 :: Taylor

My mother was being totally unreasonable, and had even blocked the computer in my bedroom. She'd had homework from school downloaded onto her Om and then had printed everything out for me. When I'd asked how I was supposed to do it without a keyboard, she told me I could read printed paper textbooks and handwrite my homework. Like, did she think we were living in the last century? Hello?

I urgently had to get through to Gabi and find out what was happening. Maybe Fergus had admitted he was the one with the juffs, or Steve had told the cops he'd brought the purple jolters, and both of them had said none of it was anything to do with me...

Yeah, that was *so* probable!

Steve—I was really upset about him. I'd thought he really liked me. So why didn't he stand up and say it wasn't true when Nessa and Delia lied to the cops, and said I was selling drugs?

There had to be some good reason why Steve didn't

take my side. Uncle Maynard would have got legal advice straight away, so maybe Steve had been told he couldn't say anything, even if he wanted to.

My eyes filled with tears. I blinked them away. I was totally not going to cry about how unfair this all was. I knew Nessa Young would be spreading stories about me all over school. I'd seen her do it before to anyone she'd decided to destroy. She was such a bitch!

Gabi was so popular with everyone that they'd listen to her when she gave them the true story. I had to get people on my side in case Uncle Maynard couldn't stop the cops from charging me with drug dealing. Gabi was my only hope. But how to get to her?

Mom expected me to stay in my room all day. Right! Like I was going to do that. I did a quick reconnoiter of the house. No one was home except Eva, and she was busy in the kitchen. There was no point in asking to borrow her Om. She'd say no, and then tell my mother I'd asked.

I knew the computer in Barrett's bedroom hadn't been activated, so it was no use to me. I went directly to my dad's study. I didn't bother with my mother's room. She changed the key to the combination door lock every few days, and I was sure she had several levels of tough security on her computer, plus I knew for sure auto-surveillance cameras went on as soon as anyone opened her door.

Dad, however, wasn't nearly as paranoid. He simply punched in his date of birth to open the door's combination lock, there were no security cameras inside, and he used a spoken password to get into his computer. It was a line from some old poem, and I'd heard him say it often enough to remember it exactly: "And the azurous hung hills are his world-wielding shoulder."

Feeling the hairs prickle on the back of my neck—Mom would totally overreact and ground me indefinitely if I got caught—I slipped into Dad's study and carefully closed the door behind me, telling myself it was worth the risk to get through to Gabi.

I spoke the line of poetry with the same intonation my father used, and got into the computer without any trouble. A menu appeared. I frowned at the monitor. There was something odd on the screen. Something about me...

::

All afternoon I'd been pacing around, feeling sad, then furious, then confused. The hours dragged by while I waited for my cousin to come home so I could get my hands on his Om. There was only one thing I knew for sure—after what I'd just found out there was no way I was going to spy on him for Uncle Maynard.

"Barrett!"

He stopped outside my door and glanced in. "Yes?" Then he looked more closely at me. "What's the matter?"

"Give me your Om. I need to use it."

"I'm afraid you can't. Aunt Kara—"

"I don't care what my mother says! This is urgent. I've got to get through to Gabi."

"I met Gabi today. She—"

He broke off as I grabbed his hand and pulled him into my room. Closing the door behind him, I said, "Please don't argue with me. Just give me your Om."

He jutted his jaw. "You'll have to tell me why. It has to be a compelling reason for me to go against Aunt Kara's express orders."

Why wouldn't he just give it to me? To my horror, I felt my throat closing and my eyes filling with tears. I tried to speak, but instead I gave a loud sob.

Barrett stared at me in consternation. "Taylor, what's wrong?"

I took a deep breath. "Nothing much. Just everything."

"What in particular?"

Telling Barrett what I'd just discovered definitely wasn't on my list of things to do, but I heard myself say, "I've just found out I'm not who I thought I was." A horrible feeling of loss and betrayal flooded through me, and I began to cry in earnest.

He put an arm around my shoulders and led me over to the chair at my desk. Then he got me a glass of water and a box of tissues from the bathroom. "I'm sorry you're upset. Is there anything I can do?"

I blew my nose hard. I must look *so* feeb. When I cried my eyes went bright pink and so did my nose. "Don't be nice to me, Barrett, you'll just make me cry more."

"All right," he said with a small smile. "Then I'll work hard at being extra nasty."

I hiccupped a few more sobs. "Talk about what you did today," I said. "It'll help me calm down."

"All right. When I got to school, Acantha Brown was assigned to show me around. She was very helpful. I didn't say anything about it to her, but now I've met Acantha, I'm wondering why she's bothering to get involved with the *Ugly-D* program."

I dabbed at my eyes. "Nobody's totally happy with themselves. That's why."

Barrett looked as if this was something he'd never considered before. "Really?"

"Don't tell me there isn't something you'd change about yourself."

He shook his head. "Nothing leaps to mind."

"What about your freckles? You can't possibly like your freckles."

"I'm used to them," he said with a grin. "It's obvious they worry you more than they worry me."

The tight feeling in my chest was going away. Now that I could think straight, I had to decide whether or not to tell Barrett about the awful things I'd discovered. To buy some time, I said, "You said you met Gabi?"

"I did. And Lorena, and Nat, and Delia, and Fergus—"

"Fergus Fysher? He was at school?!"

"Shouldn't he be?"

It was almost a relief to be reminded of something else other than what I'd found on Dad's computer.

"Jeez," I said, "this makes me *really* mad. Why am I the

one to be punished for doing nothing, when Fergus sells drugs all the time, and gets away with it?"

My anger made me feel, just for a moment, that I was in control of my own life. To feed it, I said, "Are you going to tell me Steve was there too?"

"Steve Rox? I saw him. I don't believe we're destined to be friends."

So Steve hadn't even been grounded by Uncle Maynard! I was so furious, I snapped at Barrett, "You'd better think again. Steve runs the Elites. He decides who's in and who's out. Only chance you've got to join our crowd is to get along with him."

"Clearly, then, I'm destined to be an outsider." Barrett didn't even seem to care.

Now I'd stopped sobbing like a baby, I was starting to feel embarrassed about crying in front of my cousin. I sat up straight, and, pretending to be interested, asked, "And what else did you do today?"

Barrett went through the classes he'd taken, and how Mr. Dunne had been removed from the room before the period had ended.

"Will he lose his job?" Barrett asked.

I said I hoped not, because Mr. Dunne was a good teacher, even though he had some odd anti-ad ideas, and I'd been doing well in his class. Then Barrett said how after school he'd been in Shoppaganza with Eva when ADA took over the shopping complex's sound system and the advertising screens.

"If Ads-4-Life was mentioned, my mother will have been alerted. She'll have the inside story about the man who was arrested."

"What would he be charged with?"

I knew them all by heart, having heard my parents rave on at least a thousand times about ADA and the disruption that the organization caused. "Disordering commerce and undermining the economy. It's a serious crime. And probably defamation of a corporation, for implying Fysher Pharmaceuticals was careless with the Q-Plague virus."

"So it's against the law to even criticize corporations and companies? Isn't there freedom to express what you think and feel about something?"

What a stupid question! I had to remind myself Barrett was a total stranger to the real world. "Of course there's freedom to speak your mind, just so long as you don't destroy the economy doing it."

Barrett frowned. "So why are the people who belong to ADA liable to be arrested? Aren't they just giving their personal opinions?"

"You don't understand," I snapped, wondering why I was wasting time discussing this when my whole life was in ruins. "Ask Dad. He'll explain it. Or Eva. She can tell you."

"Does Eva have anything to do with ADA?"

"Eva? That's a laugh. When we lost our last housekeeper, Uncle Maynard found Eva for us. No way would he recommend somebody on ADA's side. He *hates* them, and everything they stand for."

Barrett raised his eyebrows. "Do you hate them?"

"Me? I just think the ADA people are silly. Like, everybody knows ads aren't really true, and are just trying to get you to buy things. Since we all know this, why does ADA bother to keep telling us about it?"

"But people *do* buy what they see advertised, don't they? Why?"

I was finding it hard to concentrate on what he was saying. "I'm not sure what you mean."

"If everyone knows that advertisements manipulate them, why do they go ahead and buy the products?"

"That's just the way it is. Look, Barrett, I can't talk about this now. Okay?"

There was silence between us for a few moments, then he said, really sympathetically, "What upset you today?"

I had to tell someone, or I'd burst. Thinking I'd decide how much to say as I went along, I started with, "Because my mother took my Om and locked me out of my computer, I decided to use Dad's to contact Gabi."

"But you didn't contact her, otherwise you wouldn't be asking for my Om now. What went wrong?"

Decision time. How much to tell Barrett? I took the plunge. "I knew the password to open Dad's computer— it's a line of poetry. I found something I didn't expect in his files. When I realized what it was, I had to get out of there before anyone caught me in his office."

Unlike Gabi, who would have had a million questions, Barrett just asked one. "What was the line of poetry?"

"It's weird. 'And the azurous hung hills are his world-wielding shoulder.'"

"Gerard Manley Hopkins."

"What?"

"That's who wrote the line. It comes from a poem called 'Hurrahing in Harvest.'"

"I'll try not to forget that," I said, super sarcastic.

He grinned. "I was showing off. Sorry. Go on."

It was such a relief to tell someone, even if it was my farmie cousin.

"Truly, I wasn't trying to be nosy, Barrett, but when I saw all these files on Dad's computer under my name, I had to look at them. Wouldn't you have done that too, if you'd been me?"

I half expected him to be all goody-goody, and announce he wouldn't even be tempted to snoop through someone else's files—not that Barrett would have the faintest clue how to do it anyway—but all he said was, "Yes."

"You have to swear you won't repeat this to anyone, anyone at all."

Barrett looked at me for a long moment, then said, "I swear."

"You mean it? You really mean it?"

He looked put out that I'd doubted him. "My word is my bond. If I promise something, I keep the promise."

I thought I could trust him, but how could I be sure? At least he was family... Or was he?

He gazed steadily at me. I looked into his blue eyes, and took a deep breath.

"Okay," I said. "This is what I found..."

17 :: Barrett

That night, I couldn't get to sleep. Everything Taylor had told me kept whirling around in my head. What she claimed to have discovered was beyond horrifying. I was still having difficulty believing it could possibly be true.

From Jane-Marie's science classes, I understood to some extent the technical side of how computers worked, but had only the vaguest idea of how one would go about actually using one. Taylor, as everyone in her world seemed to be, was completely at ease with everything electronic. She'd described how she had accessed the files in her father's computer, and how his computer was linked to many others, so that, with the touch of a few keys or a voice command, specific areas of information could be moved from place to place.

Her expression bitter, she'd said, "And do you know who Dad shared my files with? Who knew everything about me? My mother's Ads-4-Life Council, Uncle Maynard, and something I've never heard of before, called UnderThought."

If Taylor had interpreted what she discovered correctly, she'd been lied to about the circumstances of her birth. She was not the natural child of Uncle Adrian and Aunt Kara, as she had always believed, but was either adopted, or perhaps related to only one of her parents.

"We aren't cousins?" I'd asked.

Taylor had looked almost desperate. "I don't know! I found my DNA profile right at the end, after I'd been through other files, but by then I was terrified someone would come in, so I only had a quick glance. There was a notation that one of my birth parents was deceased, but it didn't say which one."

Now, lying in the darkness of my bedroom, I could picture Taylor's face as she'd paced up and down, rage and grief fighting for the upper hand. Then she'd flung herself into a chair and stared up at me. "If Mom is my real mother, then you're my cousin. If she isn't, we're not blood relatives."

I'd made an effort to say something comforting. "Perhaps your parents believed they were protecting you by not telling you the truth."

Anger had dried her tears and had put steel into her voice. "And were they protecting me when they used me as a long-term experiment? Were they worrying about me when they turned me into a human guinea pig?"

"What do you mean?"

"Since I was six or seven, they've had me implanted with a series of scanning devices."

"Are you sure? Could you have made a mistake? Misunderstood what you found on the computer?"

"I didn't make a mistake," she'd said flatly. "The evidence was there—file after file. The early ones were fairly simple. The later ones, when the technology had been further developed, had multiple streams of data. Data that was all about my reactions to the world around me."

Taylor had explained how all advertisements were required to have an individual electronic signature, so when she was exposed to them, each ad was automatically identified, along with her reactions to it.

"But why?"

"There isn't any doubt why. I've been providing raw material for Dad's studies on the psychology of persuasion and my mother's work with the Ads-4-Life Council. They've used the readings I provided to rank persuasive techniques for my age group, based on how well each ad worked on me."

"But why was Senator Rox involved? And Under-Thought?"

"Uncle Maynard? *Dear* Uncle Maynard." Her face twisted. "I thought he was fond of me, I really did. But he was just using me, like my parents."

"I can't see what benefit it is for the senator to know how you react to advertisements."

"I'm not sure either, although he has a lot of business interests. And he pretty well controls the Ads-4-Life Council through Mom. There are political ads, of course.

I've often heard Uncle Maynard say how important it is for politicians to influence young minds, so that when we're old enough to vote, we vote the right way—which would be for him and his party."

"And UnderThought? What can that be?"

Taylor had shaken her head. "I've never heard the name before."

There'd been silence between us for a moment, then Taylor had given a short, angry laugh. "I'm just a lab rat, aren't I? I've been monitored for years, and never known a thing about it."

She spread her hands. "Great, isn't it? Somewhere in my body I have an electronic bug relaying everything about me to a central database."

Struggling to understand, I'd said, "Would this have anything to do with the Safety Sentinel chip everyone has inserted in their wrists? I know how it uses global positioning technology, but could it do more?"

"This has to be a lot more complicated than GPS. My implant acts as a relay station, collecting and storing information until it gets the command to pass it on for analysis somewhere else."

A cold chill had touched my skin. "Is our conversation being monitored by that bug now?"

That got a shadow of a genuine smile from Taylor. "Not unless you're a walking advertisement for some product, Barrett. And since I'm grounded, and supposed to stay in my room and stare at the wall, plus my mother has taken my Om and forbidden any entertainment, there's no way I'm exposed to any ads, so there are no identifying signatures to be picked up."

"This device in your body... wouldn't you feel it? How big would it be?"

"Tiny. It's sure to use nanotechnology."

At any other time I would have asked what nanotechnology was, but this lifelong betrayal of my cousin had filled me with outrage. "This is unconscionable! You have no privacy at all."

She'd nodded, her face full of misery. Then her expression changed to one of astonished anger. "I've just realized—when Mom and Dad yelled at me about using the GPS displacer to deceive them, all the time they knew exactly where I was. And they probably know I've tried pastel jolters a few times, because it's clear from the reports I've seen that the device takes a complete physical profile every day."

"What are jolters?"

Taylor waved my question away. "Soft drugs. Nothing important."

"Illegal drugs?"

"I suppose."

It seemed to me that any sort of illegal drug had to be important and potentially dangerous. It was clearly a serious matter to be accused of selling drugs, because this was why she was in so much trouble with the school, and maybe with the police.

I'd become aware Taylor was staring at me. The enormity of what she'd found on her father's computer seemed suddenly to have hit her.

"They've always known exactly where I was and what I've been doing. Every moment." She'd looked down at herself. "I've got to get rid of it!"

For a moment I'd thought she'd become hysterical, but I'd underestimated Taylor. Visibly forcing herself to be calm, she'd said, "We have to find someone to help us. Until we do, we have to act normally, as though there's nothing wrong. Nobody must suspect we know anything."

Later, running the scene through my head, I again got a warm feeling of acceptance at her use of "we." It seemed I wasn't her farmie cousin anymore—I was Barrett, her co-conspirator.

I was just drifting off to sleep when a thought jolted me awake. Suddenly all the questions my aunt had asked me when she came to Simplicity took on a new and dreadful significance.

I remembered Aunt Kara calling me an advertising virgin. And she'd said, "I believe I'll find your reactions to the modern world very, very interesting."

Could *I* be carrying an electronic device like Taylor's? Surely it was impossible—when could it have been implanted?

My tongue explored the tooth Dr. Selkirk had said needed urgent attention because it was decayed.

I sat up in the darkness, my skin crawling. What better

time to insert such a device than when someone was under a full anesthetic...

::

I didn't see Taylor the next morning because, like last night, Eva took a tray up to her. My cousin hadn't been allowed to leave her room, even for meals. Uncle Adrian would have been less strict, but Aunt Kara was still furious and had refused to let Taylor join us.

"In case you're thinking of popping in to visit your cousin," said Aunt Kara to me at the breakfast table, "I absolutely forbid it. Taylor has to learn to live with the consequences of her actions."

Uncle Adrian looked up from buttering his toast. "You're being a little harsh, Kara."

My aunt's face went almost as red as her hair. "Harsh! Do you know how many calls from the media I've fielded at the office? And if Maynard can't get her out of this, the stupid little fool will be charged with, at the very least, drug possession."

"Oh, Maynard will fix it," said my uncle, with a twist to his mouth, as though he'd tasted something sour. "He can fix anything."

"I'm hoping you're right," she snapped, "but if not, this will be a severe embarrassment to me."

Uncle Adrian sighed. "It's always about you, isn't it, Kara?"

Aunt Kara's eyes flashed with fury. It was obvious she

was about to give a biting reply, but then she glanced at me. "Adrian, we'll continue this discussion later. Barrett, hurry and finish your breakfast, and get ready for school."

As I left the room to go upstairs and brush my teeth—well, not exactly brush, but allow a Dentosonic to clean my teeth with supersonic sound waves—I heard Aunt Kara say to Eva, "I want Barrett exposed to megamarket products. Take him with you this afternoon when you do the weekly food shopping."

I probed my back molar with my tongue. I was convinced that was the location of the electronic bug, which no doubt would be recording my reactions to every advertisement I saw today. A wave of fury engulfed me. How dare anyone invade me like this! I hesitated outside Taylor's door. If only I could talk with her. She had to have some ideas about who we could turn to for help.

As though she could see me hesitating there, Aunt Kara called up the stairs, "Hurry up, Barrett! You've got five minutes."

In the car, Eva was silent, her face expressionless. "Are you all right?" I asked.

"I'm fine."

She didn't look fine. In fact, she hadn't looked well since the arrest of the member of ADA in Shoppaganza.

Last night, Aunt Kara had seated me in front of the entertainment wall, and stayed with me while I'd watched a series of programs. Well, half-watched them—I was too upset about everything Taylor had told me earlier to really concentrate. Every hour there seemed to be a short news segment, although it was almost indistinguishable from the other programs because it seemed to be treated as entertainment, with background music and two or three newsreaders laughing and commenting on the stories they were presenting.

What had caught my attention was an item on the ADA member I'd seen struggling with the security guards at the shopping complex.

"How 'bout that James Owen of Against Deceit in Advertising!" exclaimed one female newsreader with masses of red-orange hair piled up on top of her head. She put down the can of drink she was holding so the name on the label, Joltarema, was clearly visible. "The word is, he's retained Sholinda Haslett to defend him!"

A much larger-than-life-sized image of James Owen appeared on one side of the wall, and the face of a striking woman with a shaved head appeared on the other side.

"Sholinda Haslett!" exclaimed the other newsreader, a smooth-faced man with intense blue eyes, pointing at the bald woman. Then he grinned, showing many very white teeth as he slapped his can of drink down too. "Sholinda has so much energy, it's clear she must drink Joltarema every day!"

"If I were in trouble, she's the lawyer I'd call!" declared the woman. "Sholinda Haslett is the one!"

"She's the best! I'm betting James Owen will get off!" the man exclaimed.

Then an advertisement for Sholinda Haslett Legal Services had begun. In quick succession, a bewildering set of images of the lawyer, with people I presumed were clients she'd successfully defended, flashed on the wall. Blinking over these staccato images were the words: *The ultimate defense! All you need is Sholinda Haslett by your side!*

At this point, Aunt Kara had made a sound of disgust and turned off the wall. "Time for bed, Barrett," she'd said. "You have a demanding day ahead of you tomorrow, unfortunately without the benefit of my daughter's company."

In this noisy world I valued any wells of silence, but now, this morning, I wanted information.

I said to Eva, "I saw the ADA man, James Owen, on the news last night."

She nodded, her eyes on the road, but she didn't comment.

"He seems to have a famous lawyer representing him."

"Sholinda Haslett. She costs a fortune, but she gets results."

Uncle Paul had considered the legal system in the Chattering World to be totally corrupt. "Pay enough money, you can get away with anything," he'd said scathingly on more than one occasion.

"So James Owen is likely to be found not guilty?" I ventured.

"One can only hope so." Her tone seemed to indicate the subject was closed.

After a few moments, I said, "Will Senator Rox be able to fix things for Taylor?"

Eva made a derisive sound deep in her throat. "I'd be astonished if he doesn't."

"So why is Aunt Kara so angry with her?"

She glanced over at me. "Kara Trent has political ambitions so, understandably, it's important for her to maintain an excellent public persona. Having a child accused of drug use and dealing is not helpful, to say the least."

I sat back to think about this. "So Aunt Kara has plans to leave the Ads-4-Life Council?"

Eva paused, as if she were weighing up whether to go on, or not. At last she said, "This is the situation, Barrett. If all goes according to Maynard Rox's grand plan, the next election will see him installed as leader of the country. Everything he does and says is directed towards that purpose."

"And Aunt Kara?"

"She has a very high profile as head of the Ads-4-Life Council, so her transition to politics should be smooth, especially as arrangements will be made to have someone step aside so she can be elected. Rox will put her in charge of Medical and Health Services."

This didn't seem right to me. "But her area of knowledge is advertising, isn't it? Not medicine."

This got a cynical chuckle from Eva. "Politicians aren't appointed because of their expertise in the area in question. Loyalty to their leader is the litmus test."

She added, as we drew up at Fysher-Platt Academy's gate, "I've heard that drug companies are supporting Rox and his party to the tune of millions of dollars."

I got out of the car thinking about this. Did Eva mean to imply that Aunt Kara, should she be appointed to that position in Senator Rox's government, would help the drug companies any way she could?

::

By the time Eva picked me up in the afternoon, I was mentally exhausted. I'd spent the day in Acantha's company, and she guided me through the various classes. English was the first lesson. At the beginning, Mr. Dunne read an admission of guilt for, as he put it, "inadvertently defaming a school sponsor, Flidder Ice Cream, in yesterday's class." Although his apology was contrite, the tone he delivered it in made it clear that Mr. Dunne didn't really mean a word of it.

The rest of the day wasn't quite so daunting as yesterday had been, but the flood of names, and places I had to be at certain times—and equipment I couldn't fathom how to use—had all left me feeling rather frustrated and confused.

I hadn't seen Steve Rox, or Taylor's friend Gabi. In fact, the only familiar person I'd spoken with was Acantha. I did catch sight of Mr. Platt, whom I'd met on the first day. I would have said hello, but he glared angrily at me and hurried away, so I gathered that Eva had told Aunt Kara about him offering to be my agent, and that he'd got into trouble for it.

"Do we have to go shopping?" I said, as I got into the car. "I'm really tired."

Eva herself looked weary. "We still have to get the sports equipment and the book reader we didn't get yesterday," she said, "but that can wait. Your aunt particularly asked me to take you to the megamarket this afternoon."

I thought I knew the answer, but I said, "Why?"

Eva shrugged. "Ask her, not me," she said shortly.

Wondering if she regretted our earlier conversation in the car, I said, "About this morning—"

"Let's forget about this morning, Barrett. All right?"

"All right."

We didn't speak again until we reached an enormous building surrounded by a huge parking area absolutely packed with vehicles. On top of the building was the sign: Monster MegaMart! Stop! Shop! Save!

I'd thought we'd have to leave the car a long way from the entrance, but Eva drove to a series of parking spots close to the building. There were several empty of vehicles, but each was protected by a metal barrier. As we approached one of them, its protective barrier slid down into the ground, so Eva could park our vehicle.

"Reserved parking spot," she said. "Very expensive

annual fee, but your aunt considers it money well spent, seeing how often we shop here."

Inside, the MegaMart was as confusing as the Shoppa-ganza complex had been. The gigantic area was divided into many sections, each with corridors of shelving. Music pulsed, lights sparkled, screens exploded with pictures. Masses of people crowded the aisles with wire mesh buggies, which were also covered with scintillating advertisements.

Eva knew exactly where she was going, and I shadowed her as she set off at a brisk walk. We were heading for the section devoted to food. I gazed around, amazed, having never seen so many provisions in all my life. Boxes and cartons and packets and cans and bottles—all brightly colored, all flashing and flaring to attract attention.

Eva gestured, and a buggy came purring over to us. Like an obedient dog, it followed us closely as we began to walk the food aisles.

"Buy me! Please buy me!" exclaimed a box that, from the pictures dancing on its surface, held breakfast cereal of some sort. It was one of an overwhelming number of similar cereal boxes, each one desperately trying to catch our attention.

Eva ignored the entreaties, and homed in on one particular brand in a glossy white box, which sang with joy when she picked it up, then changed to a pleased rosy pink. It reverted to white and fell silent when she placed it in the buggy.

I leaned over to examine the box. "Eva, how does it work?"

"It's a recent development, and not, to my mind, a good one," she said tartly. "Ultra-thin, flexible color display screens are printed onto paper or foil. The technology is cheap enough to be used on throwaway packaging."

"How does it change from white to pink?"

"It uses electrochromatic substances that alter in color when an electrical voltage changes the alignment of molecules. The power for this and for the audio comes from batteries printed onto the packaging."

I wasn't surprised that Eva knew all this. I was already convinced that she was much more than a housekeeper.

"You'll see the same technology in magazines," she said. "There are racks of them at the checkout lanes. They're all starting to include flexible screens offering computer games, interactive ads, and video illustrations for articles. And if you wish, with the touch of a finger you can change the pages from English to another language."

I felt the now familiar sense of being overwhelmed by too much information. "Doesn't anyone yearn for a simple life? For quietness?"

Eva gave me a quick smile. "I do. Often. And you should talk to your uncle. I've heard him say how sorry he is that his research has encouraged advertising to become more and more frantic and intense. He'd understand how you feel."

Uncle Adrian? He seemed more moderate than Aunt

Kara, but he had used his own daughter as a tool for his research. Why would he care about me, except as a source of new information?

18 :: Barrett

Later, when I went up to bed, I paused by Taylor's door, but the sound of my aunt's footsteps coming up the stairs convinced me to continue on to my own room. It was a long time before I slept, and when I did, I was troubled by vivid, violent dreams, of which I could remember only a few disturbing fragments when I awoke, bleary-eyed, the next morning.

I came downstairs just as Eva was sent up to tell Taylor she was permitted to come to breakfast. The reason for this concession was sitting at the table with Uncle Adrian and Aunt Kara: Senator Rox. Even I could see that the gray suit he wore must be very expensive. His thick pale hair was a contrast to the tanned skin of his face.

I'd waited with some trepidation for him to say something about the difference of opinion I'd had with his son, but when the subject was never mentioned, I took it that Steve hadn't told his father what had happened.

When Uncle Adrian was engaged in conversation with Senator Rox, I took the opportunity to say to my aunt,

"I've finished a letter to my friends at Simplicity. You said you might be able to have it delivered. Would that be possible?"

Aunt Kara took the folded pages from me and turned to Eva, who was waiting for Taylor to arrive before she served breakfast. "Eva, get Lloyd in here, please. He's working in my study."

Lloyd appeared a few moments later. I'd never seen Aunt Kara's assistant, and was surprised at how young he was. He had a whippy, hard body, ultra-short black hair, and cold blue eyes.

Aunt Kara handed him my letter. "Get this to Simplicity Center. You'll have to use a courier service of some kind."

Lloyd didn't seem at all put out by her abrupt manner, which was close to rude, I thought. "Of course," he said.

Holding my letter, he stood waiting, until she dismissed him with, "That's all."

Taylor arrived as he was leaving the room. I thought her smile was forced, but nobody seemed to notice anything wrong. "Lloyd! I didn't know you were here."

"Don't interrupt him, Taylor," snapped her mother. "Lloyd has a lot of work to do."

Taylor came over to kiss Senator Rox's cheek. "Uncle Maynard! Have you...?"

"Fixed it for you?" he said in his rich, fruity voice. "Your mother tells me you don't deserve it, but yes, Taylor, I believe I have been able to intercede on your behalf."

"You're the best!"

"Very possibly." His smile included me. "In fact, I'll chauffeur you both to the Academy, just to make sure that the matter has been taken care of satisfactorily."

I had to admire how Taylor was acting towards Senator Rox and her mother. I knew how betrayed she felt, but her manner gave no hint of this, although she was very pale. I wondered if she'd had as much trouble sleeping as I'd had.

Eva, too, still seemed drawn and preoccupied. Without speaking, she served everyone a hearty breakfast of eggs, bacon, and fried potato. When she got to Senator Rox he beamed at her. "You're an angel, Eva. I've a good mind to ask you to come back with me and run my house."

Eva remained stone-faced as Uncle Adrian said with a chuckle, "Hands off, Maynard. Eva belongs to us."

Maynard Rox raised his eyebrows, saying jocularly, "What the senator gives, the senator can take away."

Looking at Eva, I thought about how I'd mentioned to Taylor that Eva had referred to her as being "closely monitored." I was sure that Eva knew about her electronic implant.

Taylor had dismissed the idea. "Why would she know about it? She's just a spy for Uncle Maynard, that's all."

"Why would she spy for him?" I'd asked.

Taylor had shrugged. "Uncle Maynard doesn't trust anybody, even my parents, who have every reason to support him."

While I was musing over this, the conversation at the breakfast table turned to rumors of an outbreak of Q-Plague.

Taylor mentioned the gossip she'd heard about some girl at a party coming down with Q-Plague.

"Unfortunately," said the senator, "even though the government takes preventative measures, it remains true that an outbreak could occur. However, this story you've heard is baseless."

"But Q-Plague kills almost everyone who gets it, doesn't it?"

"Don't worry your pretty head, Taylor. Fysher Pharmaceuticals have developed a new wonder drug, Cue-Kill. It appears to be the only viable treatment for Q-Plague." He rubbed his hands together. "Ultimately Cue-Kill will be worth billions of dollars."

Beaming at Aunt Kara, he added, "A wonderful investment for you, Kara, my dear. I'm so glad you took my advice and put considerable money into Fysher Corporation's shares. I'm predicting their value will shortly skyrocket. To cover Fysher's substantial research and development costs, Cue-Kill will be very expensive. But as the only drug of its type on the market, it doesn't need to be priced to beat the competition—there isn't any. And I can tell you, confidentially, that Fysher is about to reveal a revolutionary new memory pill, Augment, which is far superior to anything else on the market."

I'd been silent up to now, but I was curious to see what

would happen if I brought up the subject of ADA and their accusation that Fysher had released Q-Plague. "Eva and I were at Shoppaganza when ADA broke into the system and broadcast anti-ads."

"ADA?" said Senator Rox, wrinkling his nose in disgust. "Bunch of radical opportunists."

"ADA said Fysher Corporation had covered up a release of Q-Plague from their laboratories," I said.

The senator narrowed his eyes. "Anyone belonging to ADA is vermin. Extermination's too good for them."

"That rabble-rouser, James Owen, was arrested at Shoppaganza," said Aunt Kara. "He's notorious for making baseless accusations like this. He also had the temerity to attack you, Maynard, as well as the Ads-4-Life Council. Unfortunately, he's retained that Haslett woman to defend him. To counter that fact, I hope you can use your influence to make sure the man appears before a very unsympathetic judge."

Senator Rox inclined his head in the manner of some ruler granting a petition. "Consider it done, Kara."

"Can you really choose judges?" I said, trying to sound like some naïve farm boy from the country—which wasn't all that difficult. "Is that legal?"

"Strictly speaking, it's not," said Uncle Adrian. "In fact, judge-shopping is just one more corruption of the legal system."

Aunt Kara shot him a look of surprised irritation. "Adrian, it's hardly your area of expertise."

"I'm sure justice will be served," said Senator Rox, in a discussion's over tone. He gave me a broad smile. "And how are you settling in, Barrett? Finding our ways a little strange, eh?"

I agreed that I was.

"Fysher-Platt Academy will take care of that," he said expansively. "Soon you'll find yourself fitting in without any trouble." He pushed back his chair. "I'll have a word to Steve. He can make things a little easier for you."

"Thank you," I said, hiding an ironic smile. What Steve Rox wished for me had nothing to do with making my life easier. Quite the contrary.

19 :: Taylor

Uncle Maynard said he wanted a private word with my parents, so he sent Barrett and me out to wait in his limousine, his usual humungous white vehicle with darkened windows. As we approached, Will got out of the driver's seat and opened the door for us. He was looking really handsome in his navy blue chauffeur's uniform, but I'd never felt less like flirting with him.

Trying to sound as normal as possible, though the way my stomach was, I could throw up any minute, I said to Barrett, "This is Uncle Maynard's bodyguard, Will Will Do."

Will gave me a mock scowl. "Funny the first time, Princess, but now it's getting old." He grinned at Barrett. "Just call me Will."

Barrett was looking at him with open curiosity. "May I ask what a bodyguard does?"

"I do a lot of different things, but my main responsibility is to keep Senator Rox safe from harm."

"Do all important people have bodyguards?"

"Not everyone needs one, but many have them anyway." Will chuckled, adding, "A bit of a status symbol, some think."

Making an effort to stay in the conversation, I said, "It's not a status symbol with Uncle Maynard. He's had death threats and everything."

Will nodded. "Politicians like the senator make enemies. It comes with the territory. There are always citizens who feel strongly about supporting one political party and not another. That's how a democracy works."

"And is this a democracy we live in now?" asked Barrett.

Will's face went sort of blank. "Of course this is a democracy," he said.

Barrett hadn't finished with the questions. "Is Lloyd Aunt Kara's bodyguard, as well as her assistant?"

Lloyd as a bodyguard? I was about to say I'd never heard anything so dumb, when Will nodded. "Sometimes he fulfils that function."

"My mother doesn't need to be guarded," I said, shocked. "Who would want to hurt her?"

"Influential people like Kara Trent always have opponents, who criticize what they do and what they believe in. It's sensible to take precautions at those times when there might conceivably be danger." Will looked past us. "Here's Senator Rox. You'd best get in."

Uncle Maynard took the front seat beside Will. Joy! I saw my Om in his hand. "Here, my dear," he said, passing it back to me. "With some difficulty I managed to extract this from your mother. I'm afraid she's still quite angry about your deception."

My deception! What about hers and Dad's? And his, too! I was so furious I almost blurted something out, but Barrett put a hand on my arm and gave me a warning look, and I subsided. He was right. We had to play it cool. "Yeah," I said, "I'm sorry about that."

I knew I didn't sound the least bit sorry, but Uncle Maynard didn't notice. He checked his watch, then said, "Will? The news digest, please."

While Barrett gazed out the window, and Uncle Maynard watched the news in a pop-up screen with the sound funneled so only he could hear it, I tried to get Gabi on my Om. We'd been out of touch for ages, and I knew she'd have lots of stuff to pass on. And of course my news would totally blow her away.

Gabi was my best friend, but I hadn't decided whether I'd tell her or not. If it hadn't been for Barrett, I'd absolutely have to, because there was no way I would have been able to keep it totally to myself. But there was still lots to find out, so maybe I'd wait. What was UnderThought, for example?

I couldn't raise Gabi's Om, which hardly ever happened. I'd see her in a few minutes at school anyway, but I left her a voicemail saying, "Where are you? Talk to me!"

I sat back in the soft leather seat, thinking of who else I'd call, but for once I really didn't feel like contacting anyone. I glanced over at Barrett. He was a sweet guy—I had to admit it. Steve Rox wasn't half as nice.

Barrett was concentrating on what was passing by outside. I looked to see what it was. We were just coming up to one of the really giant holographic billboards. By coincidence, a Fysher Corporation advertisement was running. I tried to look at it through Barrett's eyes, as if I'd never seen anything like this before.

Happy Happy Happy was bursting in colored bubbles around a widely smiling girl's face. She looked familiar— it was Petunia Madison, who'd almost won *Worldsong*. Then, in an explosion of bright light, the words *Blissjoy! Make Life Shine Again!* began to grow larger and larger until they blocked out Petunia Madison altogether.

"Blissjoy is a mood lightener," I said to Barrett, as Fysher Pharmaceutical's logo—a purple F and P sort of tangled together, appeared.

"I know. Yesterday my science period was kindly brought to me by Blissjoy." He sounded rather sarcastic.

I gestured back at the billboard we'd just passed. "So what did you think of that ad?" I added with a grin, "Did you find yourself getting ready to run out and buy Blissjoy?"

Uncle Maynard must have heard my question, because he turned his head to say to Barrett, "Advertising is largely about emotions. What are your feelings about the Blissjoy commercial you've just seen? Do you get an impression of happiness, exhilaration?"

"I'm afraid not," said Barrett. "I get the impression I'm being cynically manipulated."

Usually Uncle Maynard would argue about how advertisements were essential to the economy, but this time he didn't respond, because something on the pop-up had caught his attention. "Here it is at last!" he exclaimed.

I leaned forward to see what had got him so excited. The sound was directional, so I couldn't hear what was being said, but the crawl along the bottom of the pop-up made me punch the activation fast to snap up Barrett's and my personal pop-ups. The sound came on halfway through a sentence.

"... severe and spreading outbreak of Q-Plague."

The newsreader was pretty old, not particularly good-looking, but with a deep, strong voice that sounded very convincing, as if he really did know what he was talking about. If the presenter I liked on *Welcome the Morning*, Tad Fortune, had been reading it, he would've made the whole thing sound like a bit of a joke, but with this guy, you knew it was serious.

"Health authorities reassure this is not an epidemic, but is restricted to a few scattered cases, and they remain hopeful this is a mild strain of the virus. Independent sources, however, reveal a much more worrying situation, with fatalities already being reported in several areas. This information has not yet been verified. Stay tuned for breaking news..."

The picture on the pop-up switched to a reporter with

the new burnt-orange hair. It didn't really suit her, and it was windy, so she had orange strands flapping all over her face. She was standing outside big wrought iron gates, and behind her masses of kids were collecting, some waving to the camera.

"Isn't that the Academy?" Barrett asked.

"It is," I said.

A ghastly cold feeling swept over me as the reporter continued, "We have confirmation that two students attending the exclusive Fysher-Platt Academy have been stricken with Q-Plague. Tragically, one has already died. The other's condition is listed as critical."

The newsreader appeared again. "Isn't it true, Jane, that Fysher Pharmaceutical Corporation have the only known drug effective in combating this dreaded virus? And that it's prohibitively expensive?"

In the front seat, Uncle Maynard exclaimed, "Prohibitively expensive! I'll have his job for that. Will, make a note to remind me to call the general manager of SatNews Digest."

On the screen Jane with the messy hair was on again. "Fysher Pharmaceuticals has spent a fortune in research to develop this new wonder drug, Cue-Kill. Supplies are being rushed to all areas where Q-Plague has been reported, including, ironically, Fysher-Platt Academy. The surviving student is being treated in the school infirmary, which is, we are assured, a state-of-the-art medical facility. And as we speak, the parents of the afflicted students are receiving professional counseling, all at Fysher-Platt's expense."

While they'd been speaking, across the top of the pop-up's screen ran: *Fysher Pharmaceuticals! Your health is our health! Proudly bringing Cue-Kill to you, the new and the only effective treatment for the devastating Q-Plague. Be fully prepared—get your just-in-case supply today.*

Then the screen split, with orange hair on one side, and the newsreader on the other. "And what vital information about Q-Plague does our audience need to know, Jane?"

"Just this, Tom: Q-Plague is a deadly virus that kills its victims within twenty-four hours from the first signs of infection—high fever, plus a red rash on the palms of hands and soles of feet."

"And how is Q-Plague transmitted from victim to victim, Jane?"

"By contact, Tom. We urge audience members not to touch any person you have reason to believe might be infected." She gave a small smile. "Tragically, kissing is not advised. The virus has been isolated in saliva."

"I couldn't get Gabi on her Om," I said to Barrett, "and she never turns it off. What if she's got Q-Plague?"

He put his hand over mine. "We're nearly there," he said. "I'm sure you'll find Gabi's all right."

Uncle Maynard's limo slowed to a crawl. A huge collection of media trucks was clustered around the gates to the school. Overhead, helicopters circled.

"Excellent," said Uncle Maynard. "Stop right here, Will."

"There's Steve," I said. He was on camera, being interviewed by a reporter wearing the very latest clothes. It was Tad Fortune, the sexy guy from the morning show. I stared at him. I'd never realized he was so short! Steve, who wasn't really that tall, towered over him.

Uncle Maynard caused a sensation the moment he got out, leaving us behind in the car. Reporters ran in his direction, and their camera operators hurried after them.

Everything looked so out of control, I said to Will, "Shouldn't you be doing something, with all those people rushing him?"

"There's no problem. No one's going to attack the senator when the media's there recording everything that happens. I'll just keep an eye on him from here."

"I've something to tell you," Barrett whispered to me. "Something important."

"What?"

Barrett glanced at Will, whose attention was on the scene outside.

"Will isn't even listening," I said.

"Let's get out," said Barrett.

To humor him, I opened the door on the side opposite to Uncle Maynard and the crowd around him. The reporters were shouting questions about what the government was doing about the outbreak of Q-Plague, and Uncle

Maynard was calmly answering. No one noticed us as we walked away from the limousine.

"Okay, what is it?" I said.

"I think I'm wired up, or whatever you call it, just the way you discovered you are."

When he explained, it made horrible sense. I'd have laughed at the idea a couple of days ago, but now I had the dreadful, hollow feeling that my life was falling to pieces, and that any number of awful things were possible.

"We've got to focus on finding someone to help us," I said.

"Have you got any ideas?"

I'd been scanning for Gabi, but still hadn't seen her. "Maybe Gabi's father. He's an agricultural scientist. You'd like him. Or one of the teachers, Mr. Dunne. I'd trust him."

There was a roar of laughter from the direction of the crowd. Uncle Maynard was entertaining everyone, like he always did when the media were anywhere near him.

Barrett's expression had hardened. "One person we can't trust under any circumstances is Maynard Rox."

"You're right. On top of his involvement in my bugging, he also wanted me to report back on exactly how *you* reacted to everything around you."

Barrett gave a snort of disgust. "He's despicable. And he's done worse than that, Taylor. I believe Rox is involved in some way with the Q-Plague outbreak. Remember how he was watching the news in the car, and he said 'Here it is at last,' as though he was expecting the Q-Plague to be mentioned? And at breakfast, when he was talking about how much money would be made by Fysher Corporation from the Cue-Kill treatment? I'm sure he owns shares in the company, like your mother does."

"What about asking Will for help?" I said, glancing over at the limousine. Will was looking our way, and I tried to look as though everything was all right by giving him a little wave. "I know he likes me."

"Liking you isn't enough. His allegiance is to the senator," said Barrett. "How about Eva?"

I shook my head. "No way. I told you, she's a spy for Uncle Maynard."

"I think Eva is connected to ADA in some way."

"That doesn't make her someone we can go to," I said. A shiver ran down my back. Who was there we could trust?

"Well, well, well. The little farmie's back, is he?" Steve had come up without us noticing him. "What rock did you crawl out from under?" he jeered.

Steve was just being totally stupid, and I felt like telling him so, but first, I'd get him to tell me the names of the two students who'd caught the plague.

"I wouldn't spend too much time with your cousin," Steve said to me, "not if you plan to stay an Elite."

Right now, belonging to the Elites didn't seem all that important to me. "Steve, who's got Q-Plague?" I said. "All I've heard is it's two students, and one has died."

"Hart is dead," said Steve, not even pretending to be upset. "And Gabi's dying."

"She can't be! Not Gabi!" The bottom of my world seemed to drop away from me and I felt as though I couldn't breathe.

"You'd better pray that Cue-Kill works," Steve said. "It's the only hope she's got."

20 :: Barrett

Taylor had broken down and sobbed, and I'd put my arm around her to comfort her. Then a bunch of her friends had come up, all looking very upset about Gabi, and Hart, who had died.

Steve Rox gave me a contemptuous glance, and sauntered off, hands in his pockets, in the direction of the crowd of media people surrounding his father. I saw Acantha standing alone, and joined her.

"They're talking about quarantining the school," she said. "Or alternatively putting everyone under house arrest until the plague's under control."

"I don't know much about the Q-Plague. Do you?"

Somehow I wasn't surprised when Acantha admitted that she did.

"My parents are virologists," she said. "I was born in Africa, where they've spent years researching tropical diseases. Mom and Dad were among the first to identify the Q-Plague virus."

"It's very infectious?"

I expected her to agree it was, but she shook her head. "You can catch the flu more easily than you can Q-Plague, but then, most strains of flu usually won't kill you, and Q-Plague almost certainly will."

I thought of blonde Gabi with her delightful smile. "What about the Fysher Pharmaceuticals drug, Cue-Kill?"

"It works. My parents have been involved with recent trials of Cue-Kill in Uganda, where Q-Plague is prevalent, and the results were very positive."

Curious, I said, "So you don't live with your parents?"

"With my grandfather. Mom and Dad are overseas most of the time."

I wondered what serious scientists like her parents would think of Acantha being a contestant in *Ugly-D to Teen Queen*.

Almost as though she could read my mind, Acantha said, "My mother says parenting at long distance is tricky, especially when I do something like trying out for a TV reality show. She and Dad weren't happy with me, and they blamed Grandfather, which wasn't fair, since I didn't tell him I was even entering the contest."

"The Teen Queen thing? I know about it."

Acantha smiled cynically. "Of course you do. Everyone at the Academy does. I've found it gives me a certain notoriety. Some even try to make friends with me so they can boast they know the inside story about the show."

I hadn't meant to ask, but found myself saying, "I don't

understand why you would do it—have strangers change you, so you don't look like yourself anymore."

She stared at me for a long moment, then said, "It's so different for boys. You don't know what it's like, Barrett, to be a girl and not be pretty. To have frizzy hair and a lumpy body."

"You're too hard on yourself. Besides, there's much more to a person than looks."

"Looks are everything. Beautiful people don't have to try so hard to be noticed, or to succeed. Everyone wants to be their friend. Life's easier for them."

Acantha indicated Taylor, who was walking towards us. "I'd be happy to be like your cousin. Frankly, I'd be thrilled to have all the advantages an attractive face and a nice figure would give me." She gave a bitter laugh. "Do you blame me so much for wanting what Taylor and Gabi and the rest of the girls in their group have?"

Before I could formulate an adequate answer, Taylor reached us. Her eyes were red, but she'd stopped crying. "How's Gabi?" I asked her.

"Gabi's not dying, like Steve said. She's still terribly ill, and can't see anyone, but thank God the Cue-Kill they're giving her seems to be working."

Taylor frowned at me. "Barrett, I've just heard from the others what happened between you and Steve the day before yesterday. Why did you *do* that? It was so feeb! You've totally blown any chance of being in the Elites."

"Barrett was defending me," said Acantha.

"I was told Steve called you a name. Was that such a big deal?"

"He called me an ugly bitch, Taylor," Acantha snapped. "And then he went to hit me. Barrett made him apologize."

Taylor was obviously disconcerted. She glanced at me, and I nodded. "It's true."

"Steve's saying Acantha started it by swearing at him."

Acantha gave a derisive snort. "How convenient of Steve Rox to forget *he* began the whole thing by making nasty comments about Barrett."

"Oh." Taylor hesitated, then said, "I'm sorry, Acantha. I'm beginning to learn not to believe everything Steve says."

"Is belonging to the Elites so important to you?" Acantha asked.

Taylor didn't answer. Looking past Acantha to where Steve and Will were striding purposefully towards us, she said, "Barrett?"

I was immediately on guard. Steve hung back a little, so Will reached us first. "I need a private word with Taylor and Barrett," he said to Acantha.

He waited until she was out of earshot before saying, "You two are to be quarantined."

"But why?" asked Taylor. "Nobody else is."

"Don't argue, Princess. Give me your Om. And I want yours too, Barrett."

I was beginning to recognize the obstinate jut of my cousin's jaw.

"Why do I have to give you my Om?" she asked. "I've just got it back."

"It has to be disinfected."

"That's so dumb! Gabi and Hart didn't touch my Om, and they didn't touch me to pass Q-Plague on. I wasn't even at school yesterday."

Will gave a long-suffering sigh. "Princess, don't make it difficult for me. I'm just following the senator's orders. He's been advised that you and your cousin have been exposed to Q-Plague. I don't know any details, so I suggest we stop arguing and go to the infirmary. Senator Rox and Principal Ms. Carmine-Bruett will meet us there. I'm sure you'll get answers to all your questions then."

Behind him, Steve Rox grinned unpleasantly. "Want any help, Will?"

"You can take the Oms. Barrett and Taylor won't be needing them."

Will held out his hand and I gave him my Om. I hardly knew how to use it, so it was no loss. Scowling, Taylor did the same with hers.

As Steve took them from Will, I said, "If the Oms are infected, and you both have touched them, aren't you running the risk of catching the plague?"

"Not a chance," said Steve. "My dad made sure everyone around him went on a course of Cue-Kill as soon as Q-Plague cases were reported."

Something was very wrong. "We were in your father's limousine this morning when the first cases were mentioned as breaking news. How could the senator have time to make sure you all were given Cue-Kill?"

Will shook his head impatiently. "Look, we can go around and around, and never get anywhere. Come with me to the infirmary, and I guarantee your questions will be answered."

I took the measure of Will. He was heavily muscled, with a thick neck and large, square hands. If it came to physical combat, he'd be a challenge for me. Besides, there was always the possibility that Senator Rox was right, and Taylor and I were carrying Q-Plague, but had not yet become sick.

The three of us, with Steve coming along behind, began to make our way through the crowds at the Fysher-Platt gates.

"Shouldn't we be worried about infecting people?" I asked Will.

He shrugged. "Don't touch anyone. It's direct contact that passes the virus on."

Inside the gates, a large servo-buggy was waiting for us. In my mind, I pulled up the location map I'd been given of the school. Appropriately, the infirmary building was in one corner of the extensive grounds, on its own private loop of roadway, isolated from any of the other buildings.

The panel on top of the servo-buggy was showing a

Cue-Kill advertisement. A patient obviously dying from Q-Plague was given Cue-Kill by someone in a crisp, white coat. In an instant, the patient was up and playing tennis while laughing coquettishly. Glancing around, I could see other buggies were also running a variety of Cue-Kill ads.

I climbed into the vehicle reluctantly. I was full of misgivings, but couldn't think of what else to do, other than go along with Will's instructions. I felt perfectly well, but it could be true that Taylor and I had been exposed to Q-Plague, but how?

Thinking back, Eva had seemed drawn and tired this morning. Perhaps she was sick, and had unknowingly infected everyone at the table. But that would also include the senator, my aunt and uncle, and Lloyd, Aunt Kara's assistant, and there was no mention of them being quarantined.

Of course, Taylor had been at the cyberparlor with her friends, two of whom, Gabi and Hart, had later come down with the Q-Plague. Could it be that Taylor was exposed to the disease there?

Space was cramped in the servo-buggy. I was squashed up against Taylor. Steve, an expression of sneering amusement on his face, sat opposite us. Will squeezed in behind the little steering wheel, which was small enough to belong to a toy car.

Taylor was sitting with her arms folded. "This is just some stupid mistake."

Will turned his head to say, "Don't worry, the senator will take care of everything."

I gazed out of the window next to me. We were the source of much interest. Those students not talking into their Oms were chattering to each other, and several pointed in our direction.

I saw Acantha close to the side of the buggy. Our eyes met, and she mouthed the words, "Is everything okay?"

Convinced it was very much not okay, I shook my head, and mouthed back to her, "No, it's not."

"What are you doing, Trent?" Steve demanded. He leaned forward to look out the window. "It's the ugly bitch. Saying goodbye to your girlfriend, are you?"

"Steve—"

"Oh, shut up, Taylor!"

"Shut up, all of you," Will growled from the front. The servo-buggy jerked into life and in a moment we were scooting along so fast the grass outside became a green blur.

The Fysher-Platt infirmary was a solid, square, three-story building, blindingly white in the brilliant sunshine. Two armed men in khaki uniforms stood by the front entrance. Seeing me look at them, Steve said, "Dad's personal security guards are patrolling the area, so don't get any ideas of making a run for it."

Will threw him a furious glance over his shoulder. "That's enough, Steve."

He took the buggy to a loading bay at the back of

the building. "Inside," Will said to us. "The senator and the principal will be here any minute now."

Steve Rox grinned. "Yeah, any minute," he said.

As I followed Taylor out of the buggy, Steve gave me a hard shove between the shoulder blades. Taylor exclaimed, and I swung around, ready to deal with him, but Will had already seized Steve by the front of his jacket.

He shook him, hard. "I've had it up to here with your meddling, Rox. I said no rough stuff. If there's any shoving to be done, I'll do it."

"I'll tell my father!"

"Fine. You do that."

Will released Steve who, red-faced, brushed himself down.

Will opened a heavy metal door. "This way, and hurry up."

Taylor and I went first, then Will. I looked back to see Steve, his face tight with anger, bringing up the rear. We entered a long, white corridor with a highly polished black floor made of a rubbery substance that muffled our footsteps. The walls seemed to be lined with some kind of white porous tiling. When I put out my hand to feel the texture, from behind me Will said, "Soundproofing. Keeps everything nice and quiet."

We turned several corners. I expected to see curtained wards and medical equipment, but there was nothing but the bare, blank walls, occasionally broken by a closed white door.

Eventually we approached a door that was as black as the floor. Will turned the handle and ushered us in. "You can wait here. Make yourselves comfortable."

As Taylor and I hesitated in the doorway, Will shoved us both into the room, then stepped back into the corridor. I heard Steve Rox laugh just as the door slammed shut. Too late I noticed there was no handle on our side.

21 :: Taylor

Barrett tried the door. "We're locked in," he said, "unless there's another way out of here."

It didn't take long to find that we were captives. The room we were in was carpeted in beige and had two beige lounge chairs, both positioned to face one of the featureless blank, beige walls. There were no windows.

There was another door, but it led to a tiny room containing only a toilet and a basin. On a narrow shelf sat a roll of toilet paper, paper towels, and a soap dispenser. High above, a narrow skylight provided illumination. I noticed there was no way to lock the door.

Apart from a surveillance unit in one corner of the ceiling of the main room, that was it—no other furniture, nothing to eat, no entertainment, no nothing.

"I don't believe it!" I raged. "Wait until the principal finds out we've been locked up this way. And Uncle Maynard. He'll be furious with Will and Steve."

I didn't sound convincing, even to myself. Barrett shook his head, and put into words what, deep down, I already knew. "I doubt the principal has any idea what's happened. And Will and Steve were just following the senator's instructions."

I flung myself down on the nearest chair. "I thought Steve was my friend."

"He's a bully, Taylor."

I looked up at Barrett, seeing him clearly for the first time. He was steady and sure: someone to have by your side when things went bad. How childish it seemed now, although it was only a few days ago, that I'd hotly resented him as an intruder in my safe little life.

"Yes," I said, "Steve is a bully. And I've known he was all the time, but ignored it. He's the most popular guy in the whole school. Everyone wants to hang with him."

The wall the chairs were facing flickered. "It's an entertainment wall," I said. "At least we can pass the time watching something."

The wall flickered again, then Uncle Maynard's magnified image appeared. I leaped to my feet. "Uncle Maynard! Why have we been locked up?"

"Please don't be alarmed," he said. "It's a regrettable necessity that you both be detained for the time being."

I saw Barrett looking up at the surveillance unit. He'd obviously realized Uncle Maynard could see and hear everything through it. Speaking directly to the unit, he said, "If we've been exposed to Q-Plague, as we were told, where are the doctors? Where is the Cue-Kill treatment? Why aren't we in a hospital ward?"

"Excellent questions, but I'm not inclined to answer them at the moment."

"It's nothing to do with Q-Plague, is it? You've imprisoned us here for another reason altogether."

"Don't," I said to Barrett. "Don't tell him anything."

"It's nothing he doesn't know already." Barrett looked back at the camera. "How did you find out, Senator, that we'd discovered we've been implanted with monitoring devices? Was there a microphone in Taylor's bedroom?"

Uncle Maynard tut-tutted. "What an odious suggestion, to invade the privacy of a young girl's room. I would never condone such a thing."

I said, "The only other time we spoke about it was outside the gates, and no one was near us." Then light dawned. I could see it like a movie in my head, Will watching us, and like a fool, me waving to him. He must have laughed to himself.

"It's called an eavesdrop unit," I said to Barrett. "Will pointed it at us, and the directional microphone picked up and recorded every word."

"Don't blame yourself too much, Taylor." Uncle Maynard's image on the wall smiled complacently. "We knew almost certainly it was you who had broken into your father's computer. After your illegal entry was logged and we were alerted, it was only a matter of time until you said enough to make us sure you understood the significance of what you'd found."

I was beginning to really hate his smug, self-satisfied

face. Why had I never seen before what Uncle Maynard was really like—that under his friendly manner and smiling conversation was something cold and horrible? "Who's *we*?" I asked. "My parents and you?"

He swept my question away with a gesture. "Later, Taylor. In the meantime, you can earn your keep. If you want food and drink, you'll do what I ask."

"And if we don't?" Barrett asked.

"You'll be very thirsty, and very hungry. It's much easier for you to follow simple instructions. All I'm asking is that you each sit in a chair and watch a few commercials. Now that's not an unreasonable request, is it?"

"So you can compare our reactions?"

"Much more than that, Barrett, although I must say the initial data we've been getting from you is very interesting. I won't discuss this further. You'll be constantly monitored, and if you cooperate, you'll be rewarded with quite delicious food and drink. If you don't, you'll get nothing."

His image disappeared, to be replaced by Fysher Pharmaceutical's logo.

Barrett and I looked at each other. "We might as well do it," I said. "It'll help fill in some time, and I'm already feeling a bit hungry."

"All right." He examined one of the chairs. "This thing's screwed to the floor," he said. "It can't be moved."

We sat side by side in the comfortable beige chairs, gazing at the Fysher logo.

"I'm sorry," I said. "You got involved because I told you what I'd found on Dad's computer. I had to share it with someone, but it shouldn't have been you."

"Who would you have told? Gabi?"

"She's my best friend. We tell each other everything." Poor Gabi, lying deathly ill in a hospital bed. I wished I could see her. A horrible thought had been lurking in the back of my mind. "Barrett, do you think Gabi and Hart were deliberately infected with Q-Plague?"

He looked at me gravely. "It's convenient, isn't it? All this publicity must help Fysher Pharmaceuticals. Two healthy young people get Q-Plague. One dies, to show how deadly it is. The other, Gabi, is treated with Cue-Kill, and survives."

I was aghast. "Why would anyone do such a dreadful thing?"

"Money and power," said Barrett. "It seems that some people will do anything to gain them."

Suddenly I felt totally hopeless. Uncle Maynard controlled everything. We were caught like animals in a trap.

"If it wasn't for me, you wouldn't be here, Barrett."

He twisted around to look at me. "Don't be sorry. I was involved the moment Aunt Kara collected me from Simplicity. I'm as much a guinea pig as you are. And I would never have realized I was if you hadn't told me about how you were being monitored."

The wall sprang to life, and the light panels in the

ceiling dimmed a bit. I checked my watch as the first Fysher advertisement came on. For the next hour we sat through ad after ad, all for Fysher products. Some were for Augment, the memory pill, but most were Cue-Kill commercials. They were all new.

Barrett watched them much more critically than I did. After each one finished, he'd name the strategy used to sell the product—sometimes it was simple scare tactics but, more subtly, some advertisements played upon our basic need to feel safe and secure, or our natural desire to protect people we cared about.

I was a bit embarrassed that I wasn't good at picking the underlying motivations because, after all, my father was an expert in the field of persuasion. I did pick the strategy used in the last ad we saw, which showed this girl being given the cold shoulder by her really attractive friends because they'd all taken Cue-Kill to be safe, and the girl hadn't. Then she did, and everyone smiled and was nice to her.

"Being in with the in-crowd," I said. "That's what everybody wants."

I'd never paid this sort of concentrated attention to advertisements before. They were always there, wherever I went, or whatever I was doing, so I usually ignored them. Although I had to admit they sort of seeped into my brain, because I often found myself singing a jingle, or recognizing a new product when I saw it in a real or virtual shop. And everyone at school always wanted the latest thing, and how would anyone know what it was, if the ads for whatever it was hadn't worked?

Only Mr. Dunne in English had ever talked about how persuasion could be a bad thing, getting people to think in certain ways without them realizing how it had happened.

"This is my dad's field, the psychology of persuasion," I said to Barrett, "but I really don't know much about it."

He grinned at me. "I, in contrast, know *all* about it. Uncle Paul had a bee in his bonnet about advertisements. He believed they were a form of dangerous indoctrination."

The entertainment wall went blank. Without any new picture appearing, a familiar voice said, "Remain seated in the chairs. I will be delivering lunch to you in the next few minutes. If you attempt to stand, I'll take it away immediately, and you'll get nothing."

"That's Lloyd!" I said. "Mom's assistant."

Until this moment I'd had the faintest, faintest hope that my mother wasn't involved in us being kept here, and that she might actually be looking for us. But that hope died when I heard Lloyd's voice. He wouldn't do anything like this without her knowing all about it.

Lloyd liked me—I'd often caught him looking at me—and maybe I could use that in some way. Perhaps get him not to close the door properly after he'd delivered the food...

A couple of minutes passed, and then the door opened.

Lloyd stood there with a tray in his hands. "Don't move," he said.

I'd opened my mouth to say, "Hi, Lloyd," when like lightning, Barrett was up and leaping across the room.

Everything seemed to happen at once: the tray crashed to the floor, Lloyd swore, and Barrett's shoulder hit him in the chest.

As Lloyd sat down hard, I jumped to my feet. We were going to escape!

"Get back," said Will, suddenly appearing in the doorway. In his hand he held a gun. A *gun!*

"Back," Will said, gesturing with the barrel to Barrett. I saw Barrett hesitate.

Will said, quite calmly, "Be assured I'll shoot you without a second thought."

22 :: Barrett

The gun Will held on me was a heavy silver revolver. I could see his finger tense against the trigger. This was no time to play the hero. I put up my hands in a placating gesture, and took several steps back into the room.

"That's sensible," he said. He glanced at Lloyd, who'd got to his feet, and jerked his head to indicate Lloyd should get into the corridor.

Will joined him, and the door slammed in my face.

"Oh, Barrett," said Taylor, her voice trembling. "Will could have killed you."

"I think I'm worth more alive than dead." I tried to smile. "At least I hope so."

Making an obvious effort to calm down, she came over to me and we both surveyed the mess on the floor. When Lloyd had dropped the tray, he'd been just inside the door, so the contents were strewn across the carpet.

I picked up the tray. It was made of some light plastic material, and didn't have much potential as a weapon.

Taylor's face was ashen. I admired the way she tried to

be laid back, saying, "Jeez, didn't Uncle Maynard promise us 'delicious food and drink' if we watched those ads? This is vending machine stuff."

Everything was prepackaged, so although a bit battered, it could be eaten. I didn't say it to Taylor, because she would have thought me paranoid, but I was thankful it was this type of food, because it was more difficult to tamper with. After all that had happened, the idea that they might try to drug us didn't seem so far-fetched.

I didn't feel much like eating, and neither, it seemed, did Taylor. We sat in our chairs and shared our supplies. There were doughy things with raisins that were nearly taste-less, little containers of cheese and crackers, and packets of crunchy yellow chunks that were incredibly salty. I drank a can of cola that reminded me of the dreadful Cluck Cluck Octo-Kola that had been my introduction to fast food.

Taylor picked at a few things, and sucked halfheartedly on a straw stuck into a plastic bottle whose label indicated it was a blend of rare, tropical fruits. Finally she said, "Do you think there's any hope they'll let us go? Or are we stuck here forever?"

I was very aware we were being overheard, and so was Taylor, because she glanced up at the corner of the room. Then she got up and yelled, "Mom? Mom! Are you there? And Dad? Are you? Let us out! Please! This isn't fair!"

Nothing happened. Taylor flung herself back in her chair. "What use is it to keep us here? We can't have the plague, because they haven't bothered to give us any treatment." She frowned at me. "And I know we found out each of us is being monitored all the time, but do you really think that's enough of a reason to lock us up?"

I glanced up at the surveillance unit, staring blankly down at us. A bleak feeling about what our future might hold swept over me. I believed we were under lock and key because of Senator Rox's involvement with the Fysher Corporation. The eavesdropping device Will had used to record us would have picked up me saying to Taylor that I didn't trust Senator Rox because of the money he had in Fysher, and because he'd known about the Q-Plague cases ahead of time, before they were a news item.

Although ADA had said the Q-Plague cases had been caused by the virus escaping from Fysher Corporation's laboratories, they hadn't gone so far as to suggest it had been deliberate. But as I'd said before about Gabi, it was so convenient to have such a stark illustration of what could happen to you and those you loved.

Several of the commercials I'd just seen suggested taking Cue-Kill to stay healthy. They said it was the only treatment available to prevent the deadly virus. If they created enough of a panic, how many doses of Cue-Kill could Fysher sell at high prices? Anyone who invested in the company was going to make a great deal of money.

For the first time I seriously wondered if Taylor and I would survive. Senator Rox was ruthless, and we posed a threat to him. If I were him, what would I do? Kill us?

My skin prickled. If Gabi and Hart had been intentionally infected with Q-Plague, why not do that to us too? Our deaths would appear tragic, but not deliberate murder.

Taylor was frowning thoughtfully. "You know, I heard Dad saying Fysher Pharmaceuticals is charging so much for Cue-Kill that only rich countries can afford it. You're out of luck if you're in some poor corner of the world."

While I was debating whether to share my dark suspicions, the wall came alive with Will's image. "It was stupid of you to attempt to escape. If either of you try anything like that again, you'll be punished. Severely."

"Punished?" said Taylor. "You're talking as though we've done something wrong. But you're the one who has. You've no right to keep us here. I demand to see my father."

"I'll ask the senator, Princess. Nothing happens until he gives the word."

Angry tears filled Taylor's eyes. "Who's *he* to keep us here?"

"He's the senator," said Will in a flat tone. "What he says, goes. I follow his orders to the letter."

I said, "You're holding us here against our will." Remembering something I'd learned from Samuel in law class back at Simplicity, I added, "Kidnapping is a serious crime."

His magnified face showed cynical amusement. "Good luck at making that stick, kid!" Will's smile faded. "Okay, you've had lunch because Lloyd managed to drop the tray inside the room, but that's the last meal you'll get unless you make an effort to earn your dinner. Another set of ads. And don't talk to each other. You need to relax and let them flow over you. They start in five minutes. If you need to use the bathroom, do it now."

"I hate him," said Taylor as Will's face disappeared. "And I used to think he was so nice." She got up, stamped across to the bathroom, and went in, slamming the door behind her.

I sat back and thought hard. Because my attempt to get past Lloyd had been unsuccessful, I couldn't count on the element of surprise next time the door opened. If there was some way to lure Lloyd or Will into the room...

When Taylor came out, I said, "Is there a surveillance camera in there too?"

Taylor's mouth twisted in distaste. "How sick would that be! I thought of it, and I looked really carefully. There's nothing." She glared at the blank entertainment wall, raising her voice to say with heavy sarcasm, "Thanks so much for that small mercy!"

I took my turn in the bathroom. Even though Taylor had said it was clear of surveillance equipment, I examined the little room closely, going so far as to get on my hands and knees to peer behind the toilet. Natural light came from the narrow skylight. Even if there was some way I could reach it, I was too big to squeeze through the frame.

Taylor was skinny, though. If she stood on my shoulders,

could she reach the skylight? Maybe with her fingertips. But, squinting, I could see no way to open it. And if she broke the glass, she still had to have the strength to pull herself through. That would be a challenge for a trained gymnast.

Besides, if we both disappeared into the bathroom at the same time, wouldn't they realize we must be trying to use the skylight to escape?

I washed my hands and splashed cold water on my face, hoping somehow to jolt some brilliant idea into being. The tray? Could I use the tray somehow?

When I went back to the other room, Taylor said, "I don't look like my mother, do I? *You've* got her red hair and blue eyes—I haven't."

I noticed when she'd been talking to Will, she'd demanded to see her father, not her parents. "You're thinking your father might be your natural parent?"

"See my chin?"

"It's a very nice chin," I said.

"It used to be like Dad's, sort of square and large. For my birthday, a couple of years ago, I had plastic surgery, and got this chin instead. That means I'm his daughter, doesn't it? And he's always cared more about me than Mom—"

"Pay attention!" said Will's disembodied voice. The wall came alive as he spoke.

This time they were all campaign ads for Maynard Rox. I had to admit the senator was very believable. He gazed from the screen with deep, fatherly concern, his rich voice filled with passion and sincerity.

My Uncle Paul, had he been there to see the ads, would have announced they used classic propaganda techniques. First, play on the deepest emotions of your audience, exploiting basic fears and insecurities by persuading them that there is a threat to their way of life, their health, their personal security, their incomes, or their families. Second, carefully select facts to support your point of view, and ruthlessly suppress any facts that contradict. Third, repeat the same message over and over, with so much assurance and apparent honesty that people are convinced whatever they're being told must be true.

Taylor looked wistfully at the wall as the last ad faded away. "I used to think Uncle Maynard was just terrific. Not anymore. Now everything's ruined..."

Her voice trailed off as we both heard someone at the door. It opened for an instant, and a man was pushed into the room. The door closed quickly behind him.

"Dad?" Taylor hesitated, then rushed into her father's arms. "You've come to take us home!"

He gave her a hug, then, looking over her head at me, said, "I'm sorry, both of you, that's not possible yet. I insisted on seeing you in person to make sure you were okay."

Taylor looked up at him in disbelief. "But *why*, Dad? Why are we being kept here?"

"I'm not entirely sure. It's a national security matter. I'm sure Maynard and your mother will explain it all, when you're home."

She drew away from him. She said, with a tremor in her voice, "My mother? But she *isn't* my mother, is she?"

Uncle Adrian's face was pinched and gray. "Taylor, you should never have raided my files."

She swallowed, then said so softly I could hardly hear her, "They were about *me*. I had every right to see them, didn't I?" She looked at him intently. "Dad? You *are* my father, aren't you? My real father?"

He nodded wearily. "Yes."

"But she isn't my mother?"

He stood there silently, then took a deep breath. "No, Kara's not your biological mother. It was... a genetic decision. I can't go into it now. I promise that later, you'll know everything."

Halfway between tears and anger, Taylor said, "I want to know now!"

Then the door swung open. We all turned and saw Will, his hand very obviously in his pocket, holding, I was sure, the silver revolver. "Time's up, Professor. Your wife's waiting for you outside."

"Of course." Uncle Adrian moved to give Taylor a farewell hug, then surprised me by extending his hand to shake mine. "Goodbye, Barrett, for the moment. No doubt we'll see each other soon."

Will bustled him out of the room, and the door shut decisively on both of them.

Taylor looked devastated. "Why couldn't we go with him?"

I didn't answer. The paper Uncle Adrian had passed to me in our handshake was burning a hole in my palm.

23 :: Barrett

I went into the bathroom again, amusing myself for a moment with the thought that those watching us would soon start to believe I had a bladder problem.

The note was folded into a small square. I carefully opened it out. Uncle Adrian had obviously scrawled the message in haste, as I had some trouble deciphering the words.

Doing everything possible to get you out. May take some time. I'm not alone—have help, and media very interested, but building quarantined, so denied access. You may be moved. Keeping watch so will know if you are. Rox has the authorities believing Q-Plague epidemic starting. I'm convinced not true.

He ended the note with: *Be patient.*

What chilled me was the mention that Taylor and I might be moved. Where to? A prison? A laboratory? With our electronic implants, we were already being treated like experimental guinea pigs. Why not take us somewhere more suitable for further, more rigorous research? A place where Uncle Adrian, and whoever he had helping him, could not follow?

A further chilling thought hit me. Could we trust Taylor's father? What if this was another setup? What if he only appeared to be on our side?

I put the note on the edge of the washbasin where Taylor couldn't fail to see it, and went out into the room.

"Don't be upset," I said, going over to her. Positioning myself so my back was to the surveillance unit, I mouthed the words, "Something in there." Then I said aloud, "Your eyes are all red and puffy."

She caught on fast, responding sarcastically. "Oh, thanks, Barrett! Like I care. But to please you, cousin dear, I'll wash my face in cold water. Will that be okay?"

I shrugged. "It would probably help."

She rolled her eyes, and stalked into the bathroom.

I wandered around the room, hands in pockets, now and then pausing to kick the toe of my shoe against the base of the wall.

Taylor, her face carefully blank, reappeared. "What are you doing that for?" she said. "Aiming to kick your way out, are you?"

I yawned and stretched. "I'm *so* bored," I said. It wasn't true—my mind was churning out possible escape scenarios at a furious rate. "There's nothing to do, except wait around for something to happen."

I glared at the blank entertainment wall. Raising my voice, I announced, "And I refuse to watch any more stupid, manipulative commercials, so don't bother to put them on."

Taylor suddenly wailed, "We'll never get out of here!" and put her face in her hands, her shoulders heaving. She was giving me a cue, I realized, to comfort her, so that we could communicate without being overheard.

"Don't cry," I said. I put my arms around her, conscious of how slight she was.

Sobbing loudly, she pressed her face into my shoulder. "Oh, God, I don't know whether to trust Dad," she whispered. "I want to, but..."

"I don't know either," I whispered back. "It's possible the note is just to stop us from trying to escape."

"What do you think?" she asked. "Shall we wait and see what happens? Maybe he can get us released."

"Can we take that chance?" Suddenly I was aware that Taylor was *not* my first cousin, and that, however desperate our situation, part of me was enjoying the sensation of having her in my arms. "I don't think we should wait," I murmured. "I vote we at least try to get out of here."

Taylor sobbed audibly a few times for effect, before whispering, "Got a plan?"

"Yes." In a few hasty, whispered words, I told her.

"Barrett, you could be hurt."

"Well, hello, young lovers!" Will's sarcastic voice floated in the room. "Break it up."

Taylor leaned up to kiss me. I felt my heart jump. It was

part of our pretence, of course, but just for a moment, I imagined she really meant it.

Against my lips, she said softly, "Leave this to me."

She stepped out of my embrace, wiping her cheeks with her fingers, as if she had genuinely been crying. Taking my hand, she glowered at the surveillance unit. "Let's go where we can have some privacy."

She tugged me into the bathroom. As soon as the door was shut, I said urgently, "You know what to do?"

"Yes, but Barrett—"

"I'm sure there'll be two of them. Whatever happens, if you can get out, go! Don't worry about me."

There was so little room we had to stand close together, and as Taylor opened the door a crack, I saw her hands were shaking. "How long do we have, before they arrive?" she asked.

"Depends how their minds work," I said. "If they think we're trying to break out through the skylight, I'd say they'll be here any minute. But if they think we're..." I could feel my face getting red. "You know what I mean..."

Taylor managed a faint smile. "You don't have to spell it out."

We both heard a noise at the outer door.

"They're here," I said, my skin tingling with apprehension. "Ready?"

She touched my hand. "Ready."

::

When Will burst into the room, he found me standing defiantly, blocking the bathroom door. I'd expected Lloyd to accompany him, but it was Steve Rox.

"You little bastard!" Will snarled at me. "Get out of the way." He looked back at Steve, who'd halted in the doorway. "Think you can guard the door and keep him under control while I get Taylor?"

Steve gestured with the silver revolver. "I can with this."

Will shoved me so hard I stumbled and nearly fell. He pushed the bathroom door, but it didn't move. Inside, I knew Taylor had her back against the door and her feet braced against the opposite wall, hoping to keep Will occupied at least for a few moments.

He put his shoulder against it. "Jesus!" The next time it gave a little.

Steve, smirking, was watching Will, not me. I took three great strides across the room, on the way snatching up the plastic tray I'd left handy on one of the chairs.

Startled, Steve raised the heavy gun. "Get back!" The barrel wavered.

Panic sweeping across his face, Steve pulled the trigger. The gun kicked in his hand, the shot went wide. As I reached him, I was conscious of my ears ringing from the ear-splitting, flat slap of sound.

This was no time for niceties. As Steve brought the gun to bear on me again, I used the edge of the tray to hit him across the bridge of his nose.

The tray shattered into shards of plastic. Steve bellowed and went down, blood spurting from his face onto the beige carpet. The revolver spun away across the floor, coming to rest after bouncing against the wall.

I leaped for the weapon and picked it up, but then Will collided with me. He seized my wrist in a vise-like grip, grinding out between clenched teeth, "Give it up, kid. You're out of your league."

We struggled, panting. I caught sight of Taylor, looking down at Steve, who was rolling around in pain, his hands clamped to his face.

"Taylor! Into the corridor. Run!" I shouted. I'd realized Will was the stronger, and would soon have the gun twisted out of my fingers. "Get out! Now!"

Taylor moved, but not towards the door. Will cursed as she raked his eyes with her fingernails.

He twisted his head away, to avoid being blinded. "Bitch!"

I didn't have much room to maneuver, but I managed to pivot on one foot, so I could snap-kick Will's knee with the other. I wished I'd had my boots on, but my shoes were adequate. There was an audible crack as his patella fractured.

At Simplicity I'd once seen someone kicked in the knee by a fractious cow, so I knew such an injury was crippling agony. Will released me, clutching at his leg, screaming in pain.

I grabbed Taylor's hand and together we rushed out of

the room, slamming the door behind us. "We've done it!"
she gasped exultantly.

"We aren't safe yet."

Giddy with freedom, Taylor laughed. "I'd like to see
who could stop us now!"

24 :: Taylor

I felt like we'd been in that horrible room forever, so when we came out of the infirmary at the same loading dock where we'd entered the building, it was a shock to realize it was late afternoon of the same day we'd been locked up.

As we hesitated at the door, wondering which way to go, there was a shout. I looked back to see Lloyd dashing down the corridor behind us.

Barrett and I jumped off the edge of the loading dock, and began to run. At the same time, two armed security guards came rocketing around the side of the building.

"Stop or we'll shoot!" one bellowed.

"They wouldn't dare," I yelled to Barrett. "Keep going."

We ran, with me half expecting to feel the blow as a bullet hit my back. I was gasping for air when a servo-buggy came whizzing over the grass towards us.

"Get in!" yelled my dad.

Barrett and I locked eyes, the same question in our minds. I glanced over my shoulder—one of the guards had almost reached us.

"Get in!" I screamed to Barrett.

We scrambled through the sliding door into the buggy just as the guard snatched at my arm. "Stop!" he shouted.

The buggy accelerated so hard Barrett and I fell in a tangle on the floor.

"That was close," Dad said. "I had someone watching every exit of the infirmary, in case they tried to spirit you away. Never thought you'd manage to escape by yourselves." He bumped onto a roadway. "You can tell me how you managed it later."

"Where are you taking us?" Barrett asked.

"Somewhere safe."

I clambered into the seat beside my father. Looking back, I saw the guard who'd nearly caught us had been joined by the other man. They were staring after us. "What if the guards call ahead and have us stopped at the gate?"

Dad half laughed. "We won't be stopped!" I'd never seen my father so alive. He grinned over at me. "The media's at the front of the school in force. Best protection we could have."

Barrett's face was taut with suspicion. "Why would the media be on our side? Wouldn't they always support Senator Rox?"

"The media enjoys blood sports," my father said. "If

there's a hint that a Titan might be wounded, or even fall, they want to be there for the kill."

The wrought iron gates of Fysher-Platt Academy were standing wide open. Outside, practically taking up the whole area, were masses of people. When we got close, I could see rows and rows of media trucks, even more than there had been in the morning when we arrived. A speaking platform had been set up, and huge lights were being positioned to focus on it. A bank of screens surrounded everything. Music was playing, and the screens were showing life-enhancing stories, which were really long ads made up as mini dramas.

"What's this about?" Barrett asked Dad.

"Maynard's called a media conference to detail how the government's dealing with the Q-Plague epidemic." He gave a pleased grunt. "He's expecting this to be a real boost to his career, but there's a good chance it will blow up in his face."

"How?" I asked.

"ADA has a choreographed demonstration planned, made specifically for television coverage. At the same time, they'll hack into the audiovisuals on the screens with ADA anti-ads."

"Why would that bring Rox down?" Barrett asked. "He'd laugh it off."

My father steered the buggy into a special parking area where they were automatically recharged after use. "Maynard doesn't know this yet, but I'll be releasing a written statement to the media, detailing all I know about Maynard and his covert partnership with Fysher Pharmaceuticals."

I stared at him. "What about Mom? Won't she get caught up in it too?"

My father looked away. "Kara will have to take her chances."

Then he turned back. "It's going to be a difficult time for us all. The two of you are lined up for media interviews. Also, I'm arranging for legal representation for you both. If the authorities don't move against Maynard and those working for him with a charge of unlawful detention—and they may not, because of his position in the community—we'll bring a civil suit against everyone associated with your kidnapping."

When we got out of the buggy, he said to Barrett and me, "Blend in with the crowd, but stay near the front. I'll find Lander, and bring him to you."

"You mean Fritz Lander?" I asked.

My dad raised his eyebrows. With an effort at light-heartedness, he said, "Well, wonder of wonders, you *have* paid some attention to current affairs, Taylor. I confess I'm surprised."

I tried to match his tone. "Hate to disappoint you, Dad, but the reason I know him is because he came to Fysher-Platt on Career Day to tell us all about working in the media. He's a friend of Uncle Maynard's."

"I don't think that friendship is going to survive."

Dad went off into the crowd, and Barrett and I stood together, looking around. A whole bunch of kids were getting onto the stage, and being arranged in rows at the back, with some sitting and some standing, as if for a class photo.

Barrett waved to someone near us. It was Acantha, the *Ugly-D* girl. She came hurrying over, looking mega pleased.

"You got away!" Her smile included me. "That's terrific."

Barrett was just as delighted to see Acantha. "I know it must have been you who got the word to Taylor's father that we were in the infirmary."

She nodded. "This morning, when you and Taylor were in the buggy, and I realized something was wrong, I went directly to Mr. Dunne and told him I thought you were in trouble. So Mr. Dunne asked around, and found out where you'd been taken. Then he went to Eva—"

"Eva?" I said. "You mean *our* Eva?"

"Uh-huh."

"How does Mr. Dunne know Eva?" I asked.

"She belongs to ADA. So does Mr. Dunne." She gave a small grin. "So do I."

Barrett had hinted at Eva belonging to ADA, but no way could it be true!

"I don't see how this can be possible," I said. "Uncle... Senator Rox has known Eva for ages. He recommended her as a housekeeper to my parents."

"I guess it can come out now," Acantha said. "Eva's been working for ADA for years. She got herself into your house so she could find out stuff about your mother and the Ads-4-Life Council. So, when Mr. Dunne told Eva what had happened, she told your father."

Up front, a microphone came to life. Principal Carmine-Bruett, showing off her stick legs in just about the ugliest purple dress ever, was on the platform.

"Thank you for your patience. We'll be beginning in just a moment. In the meantime, I'll take this opportunity to..."

"Oh, groan," I said to Barrett. "She'll drone on about Fysher-Platt Academy, like, forever."

He wasn't listening. "Your mother and Senator Rox are here." He pointed to where they were waiting by the stage.

I gazed at the woman I'd believed to be my mother, and felt sick. "She's not my mother," I said. "Remember?" Overhearing this, Acantha gave me a puzzled look.

As my mother—what else could I call her?—went up the steps to the platform, the TV lights all came on so everything was bathed in a brilliant glare. There were TV cameras all over. I noticed one near us was taking panning shots of the crowd. On the screens, a huge, magnified version of my mother appeared, each taken from a different angle.

Everyone quieted down as she began. "Firstly, welcome to the Fysher-Platt students behind me, who are sharing this great day with us. Now, I am honored, speaking on behalf of the Ads-4-Life Council, at this time of great challenge, when our moral fiber is tested by the deadly Q-Plague virus, to be associated with Fysher Pharmaceutical Corporation's groundbreaking public service campaign to ensure that everyone in our great nation has access to Cue-Kill, the only effective treatment for this lethal disease."

A whole lot of people clapped. I heard Acantha say to Barrett, "I've got to join the ADA people to get ready for the demo."

As she was leaving, Dad turned up with Fritz Lander. He was exactly as I remembered him from Career Day, a bony, dark-haired man who reminded me of a greyhound, although I'm not sure why. Maybe it was his long, thin nose.

"I'm delighted to meet you two brave young people," he said to me and Barrett. He had one of those super-fast smiles that come and go almost before you can see them. "Later, we'll be doing a full interview with you both about your recent experiences. It should dovetail well into the groundbreaking investigative program we're doing about corporate fraud and the buying of politicians."

"Groundbreaking?" said Barrett. "Why haven't you done a program like this before? Hasn't the corruption been going on for a long time?"

Mr. Lander blinked at him. "Well, son, you wouldn't quite get the situation, coming, as I understand, from some cult place." He flashed his lightning smile. "And that, by the way, has the makings of a superb program—your strange upbringing—"

"You were saying about the program...?" Barrett said, interrupting.

"We haven't had this kind of evidentiary material before, from so many sources, including ADA. And, of course, we have you two young people for the human interest angle. A young man and woman courageously facing together entrenched political and corporate power. What a story!"

Only days ago, I would have thought it was cool to be on television. Now it just was something to get through.

Up on the stage, my mother was speaking again. "And I am again honored, deeply honored, to be introducing to you someone who needs no introduction: Senator Maynard Rox!"

A louder round of applause this time, as the senator—I never wanted to call him Uncle Maynard again—bounded up onto the platform, acting as if he was young and full of energy. I remembered him once telling me how first impressions were vital when persuading people to like you. "Give an impression of youth and enthusiasm," he'd said. "Make them like you, because if they do, they'll do anything to please you."

On the platform, the senator was doing his arms-extended thing, as if he'd hug everyone if he got the chance.

"Thank you! Thank you! As my dear friend, Kara Trent

of the Ads-4-Life Council has said, Fysher Corporation has undertaken to provide Cue-Kill to every man, woman, and child who potentially could be exposed to mortally toxic Q-Plague virus. And that would be everyone."

Applause.

He gestured to the students standing behind him. "These fine young people sharing the stage with me are witnesses to an historic point in medical-political relationships. This will be the first time a private company and an elected government have agreed to work together to eliminate a dreadful threat to our nation—an epidemic of deadly Q-Plague. Fysher's factories are working 24/7 to produce enough of the necessary drugs for everyone."

More clapping and a few cheers this time. Suddenly I noticed a man just ahead of us hold up a placard with the words on the back so the TV cameras could read them: *There is no Q-Plague epidemic. It's a lie!*

A couple of security guards headed his way, and he put down the placard and slipped away in the crowd. On the other side of the crowd, I saw several more placards go up.

The senator held up his hands for silence. "It's only fitting that here at the prestigious Fysher-Platt Academy, where the first heartrending cases of Q-Plague have been reported, and indeed"—his face went all sad—"the first tragic death occurred—a fine young man who was at the threshold of adulthood..."

He stopped to shake his head. "Forgive me, but such

a tragic waste of young life affects me deeply." A pause, then he went on, "As I was saying, it is only fitting that I announce here, at Fysher-Platt Academy, Fysher Corporation's joint venture with our government. Your tax dollars at work, investing in the future of our great land, by providing enough of the Fysher wonder drug, Cue-Kill, to ensure that no one need suffer the horror of seeing a loved one die from Q-Plague."

Barrett was looking totally disgusted. "That man is such an appalling hypocrite. Someone should get up and tell everyone what he's *really* like."

All at once, Mr. Lander looked super keen. His long nose sort of twitched. "What an excellent idea that is! This will be a wonderful, spontaneous moment. Two young people who have shared a life-altering ordeal, getting up in front of the world to accuse the senator."

Looking me over, he said, "You're very photogenic, my dear." He peered at Barrett's face. "Pity about the freckles, but there's no time for makeup."

Mr. Lander stepped between us and took our arms. "I'll leave you at the bottom of the steps to the platform. Don't go up while there's applause. Wait until the senator is speaking, and every eye is on him."

He pushed us through the crowd, saying, "Media. Media. Urgent."

It was amazing, the way everyone moved out of the way, including the security guys guarding the speaking platform. They seemed to know Mr. Lander, because he whispered a few words to them and they nodded, agreeing with whatever he said.

"Don't worry about security taking you off the stage," he said to us. "I've told them you're part of the presentation."

As we stood waiting, Mr. Lander looked us over. "You'll do. Now, remember, you have to create a sensation. Do something dramatic. Repeat the accusation, but keep it simple. People don't like it complicated."

25 :: Barrett

I took a deep breath, ready to take on Senator Rox and expose him for what he was. Glancing down at Taylor, I was surprised to see she looked really nervous. Wasn't this what she was used to all her life? Noise and crowds and people always trying to persuade you to believe something?

"Barrett," she said in a low, urgent voice, "we can't mention we've been experimented on, at least not until we have the chance to talk to my parents."

"Why not?" I said. "There can't be anything they'll say that will excuse it."

She put a hand on my arm. "Please. I'd like to hear Dad's side, at the very least."

Fritz Lander, who'd been concentrating on what was happening on stage, turned and tapped me on the shoulder. "Get ready."

"All right," I said to Taylor. "I won't mention it."

"Go!" said Fritz Lander.

We ran up the steps. Senator Rox was in mid-sentence.

He broke off as we reached the center of the platform. His eyes widened in shock, but he managed to say, "You're interrupting an important address to the nation. Please leave."

"My name is Barrett Trent," I said, turning to the crowd. Remembering what Mr. Lander had just said, I pointed dramatically at the senator. "This man has lied to you all, for his own gain. Senator Maynard Rox has lied to you, over and over again. He has lied about the epidemic of Q-Plague. He has lied to you about his involvement with Fysher Corporation."

There was a growing murmur in the crowd. I wasn't sure whether it was for us, or against us. Senator Rox was looking around wildly. "Security? Security!"

Being much taller than him, it was possible to put my hand on his shoulder and hold him in position beside me. I had the fleeting thought that all Uncle Paul's lessons in persuasive techniques and propaganda were finally paying off.

"Senator Rox has told you how grieved he is that anyone should die of Q-Plague. He has told you everyone must take Cue-Kill to avoid infection. But has he told you how happy he is to manipulate you into believing there is an epidemic? Has Senator Rox told you about the fortune he will personally make if you are all panicked into using Cue-Kill?"

There was a louder buzz from the crowd. I felt an unexpected exhilaration. I caught sight of myself on one of the screens—a giant me looming over everything, my red hair flaming. In comparison, Senator Rox looked almost insignificant... until he spoke.

His rich voice, dripping with sincerity, rang out. "I find it truly tragic to see a young man like this, with so much life before him, demonstrate so clearly he is mentally unbalanced."

"Am *I* unbalanced too, Senator Rox?" Taylor actually pushed him out of the way so she could take center stage. To the crowd she said, "My name is Taylor Trent. You have just heard my mother, Kara Trent, introduce Senator Rox to you. Senator Rox has been a friend of my family for as long as I can remember."

She paused, turning to send him a look of utter scorn. "I called him Uncle Maynard. I thought he cared for me."

Then, turning back to the murmuring audience, her voice trembling with outrage, she said, "This morning the man I called Uncle Maynard had me kidnapped! Taken and locked up, along with my cousin, Barrett Trent. Why? Because we knew too much about his schemes."

There was a commotion next to the platform. Taylor's mother was arguing vehemently with the security guards. As I watched, she broke away and came rushing up the steps.

"Taylor! Stop immediately! You're a disgrace to—"

She never completed the sentence. With a blast of sound that drowned out everything, the ADA demonstration began. Each of the screens surrounding the area showed different images of Senator Rox, obviously when being interviewed or at public meetings. His hugely amplified words united in a garbled cacophony of sound, and superimposed over every face were the words: *Do you trust this man? He lies!*

26 :: Barrett

I thought I'd gained some concept of what the media was like in the Chattering World, but as the scandal broke, I realized I'd had only the vaguest idea of the reach and power of the entertainment and information industries.

Fritz Lander was not alone in scenting blood. A veritable pack of media hounds was soon after Senator Rox. Formerly greatly favored as a friend of the communication industry, overnight he'd become their quarry. If I hadn't despised the senator so much, I might have felt a touch of sympathy for him.

Investigative reporters scanned every utterance, checked every lead, revealed every wrongdoing—even going so far as to turn up evidence that Maynard Rox had indulged in widespread cheating, both at school and at university, and did not deserve the academic success he'd claimed.

While the media bayed at Senator Rox's heels, law enforcement took a keen interest in his affairs. Detaining us against our will had been serious enough, but the web of questionable political and business dealings he'd woven seemed set to bring about his total downfall.

The Fysher Corporation was under investigation, as were Aunt Kara and the Ads-4-Life Council. Will, Lloyd, and to a lesser extent, Steve Rox, had been charged with our false imprisonment, and all—even Maynard Rox's son—had agreed to give evidence against the senator in hopes of obtaining lighter sentences.

::

To my chagrin, I didn't escape the media's attention, either. I was torn between amusement and horror to find that a telemovie, professing to be the story of my life, was being made without consulting me, and certainly without gaining Simplicity's permission. It had been given the extraordinary and inaccurate title of *Barrett Trent: The Fish out of Water Who Turned into a Shark*.

When I complained to Fritz Lander, he laughed, saying, "The best thing you can do, Barrett, is get the true story out first, in the form of a documentary. Coincidentally, I have a project in the works myself, and I'm sure you'd be happy to be involved with it. I have the perfect title, *Innocent Avenger: The Barrett Trent Story*. All you need to do is assign the rights to your story to me."

"I don't think so."

Not at all offended, Fritz Lander grinned as he put up his hands in surrender. "Okay, you drive a hard bargain. I'll give you co-producing credit, and of course, apart from an after-sale percentage of the profits, you'll be paid up front for the rights to your story."

Thinking of all the money I was determined to repay to my aunt and uncle, I said, "I'll consider it. I believe I need to consult with a legal person first."

Lander laughed some more. Clapping me on the shoulder, he said, "You're a fast learner, my boy, a fast learner."

::

Taylor and I were anxious to learn the details of how Maynard Rox had been involved with her father and purported mother, and how Rox had used the research our implants had provided. We sat in Uncle Adrian's study while he explained what had happened over the years.

Kara Trent had known Maynard Rox prior to his entry into politics, and, sharing his taste for power and influence, had willingly been drawn into his business and political activities, however questionable.

Uncle Adrian, long before he became a professor, had also been associated with Maynard Rox, and although he resisted anything that was clearly illegal, he confessed to turning a blind eye to some dubious activities. "I fell into the trap of assuring myself that the end justified the means," he said to Taylor and me, "and that, in order to succeed, Maynard was forced to use the underhand methods common in politics."

Rox had encouraged him to aim for the higher reaches

of the academic world, correctly assuming that not only would my uncle's research on persuasion be of great value, but that it would reflect well on Rox to be associated with such an accomplished scholar.

When Adrian Stokes fell in love with Kara Trent, Rox encouraged the union, seeing it as a way to tie my uncle more tightly to him, as well as providing an opportunity to create a perfect family for Rox's secret research purposes, which went much further than the simple application of advertising strategies to political advertising.

When it was found that Kara Trent could not bear children, a young woman, a former research subject chosen by Rox, was well paid to be inseminated with Adrian Stokes's sperm, and carry the baby to term. After Taylor was born, the woman vanished. Now there was an active investigation into what had happened to her. So far no trace had been found, and there was even a suggestion that Maynard Rox may have been involved in her disappearance.

Kara Trent took over as the baby's mother, and when Taylor was seven years old, she allowed the little girl to be fitted with the first of a series of increasingly sophisticated implants, thus unknowingly becoming a subject of ongoing, intensive research.

"Oh, Dad," said Taylor. "How could you have let that happen?"

Looking wretched, he said, "I'm so sorry. I can only ask you to forgive me, Taylor. For a long time I reassured myself the implants weren't hurting you in any way, and besides, Kara and I agreed the data we obtained from you was fascinating."

"When I was older, you should have told me!"

He reddened under her accusing stare. "If it's any comfort to you, I became increasingly uneasy about the situation, and I demanded your implants be deactivated. Both Kara and Maynard said emphatically that this was impossible. Maynard delivered a not-so-veiled threat, pointing out that someone in my position had a great deal to lose if it became public knowledge that I'd been party to such unethical research on my own daughter."

"What about me, Uncle Adrian?" I said. "Did you know Aunt Kara had arranged to have a device put in my tooth?"

He moved uncomfortably. "I'm very sorry to say I did."

"And you didn't do anything!" Taylor exclaimed. "You always went along with what my mother and Senator Rox wanted, like asking me to spy on Barrett. Is that it?"

Shamefaced, he nodded. "Until I discovered this week what the UnderThought Project is. I'd noticed the name before, and thought it was just one of Maynard's political sites."

Taylor and I looked at each other. UnderThought had been one of the destinations for the files containing the data from her implant.

"What is UnderThought?" I asked.

"I'll get Eva," said Uncle Adrian. "She was the one who alerted me, and can explain it better."

When my uncle left the study, Taylor said to me, "I don't know if I can really forgive Dad."

"He saved us."

She sighed. "But even so...."

I had the bitter thought that at least she *had* a father. Mine had died before I was old enough to know him. "Taylor, he's your father, and he loves you."

"And I love him, but how can I ever trust him again?"

I was surprised to find myself defending Uncle Adrian, but I was coming to the conclusion that he'd been weak, rather than evil. And he'd apologized, which was more than Aunt Kara had done. I said, "What he did was very wrong, but he's deeply ashamed, and he's said how sorry he is."

"Maybe you're right."

She broke off as Uncle Adrian and Eva came into the study. Eva was smiling. She'd told us earlier that the authorities, influenced by the wave of public support for ADA, because now it was clear that so much of what the organization had been saying was true, had reduced the charges against James Owen. Now his offence was merely a simple misuse of Shoppaganza's electronic systems, so he'd been released from custody and faced only a fine.

Eva's smile faded as she said, "You want to know about UnderThought. It was to be kept totally secret—

understandably, since there'll be an uproar when it gets out what it involves."

Eva went on to say how ADA had been monitoring Maynard Rox's activities for some time, and had come across intriguing references to something called UnderThought. "We used our best operators to try to crack the various encryption devices. Last week we finally broke through, discovering that UnderThought is an entity created by Rox with the explicit purpose of developing advanced brainwashing techniques, specifically directed towards influencing young people like you."

"Why us?" asked Taylor.

"Because you belong to the age group most prized by big business," Eva said. "The theory is that the brand names you choose when you're in your teens or early twenties are the brand names you'll continue to buy throughout your life. Advertising people refer to it as product allegiance."

"I don't believe it. We're not that stupid."

Eva gave Taylor a bleak smile. "I'm afraid the research shows that it's true. We've come a long way in the twenty-first century. Advertising campaigns are more successful because the psychological buttons to push are so much better understood. UnderThought has gone one step further, using data from you, and then from Barrett, along with other research, to develop a series of hidden manipulative techniques with a frightening level of effectiveness. To conceal his involvement, Rox has set up a dummy company to secretly market UnderThought to corporations at a premium price, with the guarantee that it will have an astonishing impact upon the buying patterns of the young audience they so prize. The senator stands to make a fortune."

Uncle Adrian said, "I knew nothing of this until Eva came to me. She believed your lives were in danger, so she took the chance that even if I had been involved with UnderThought, my concern for you would be the overriding factor."

My uncle confronted Aunt Kara and she confirmed that UnderThought existed. My aunt said that she endorsed everything Maynard Rox was doing, and supported any drastic steps he might take to protect the UnderThought project.

"I let Kara think that, as usual, I'd go along with her and Maynard," said Uncle Adrian, adding with a bitter smile, "She never doubted I would, but for once, she was wrong."

::

Taylor and I discussed whether we should tell anyone about our implants. To protect Taylor's father, we agreed not to mention them. Uncle Adrian arranged to have the devices removed, but not by Dr. Selkirk, who'd been charged with various ethical breaches, and had his license to practice revoked.

Now that everything was in the open, my Uncle Adrian and Aunt Kara had separated, preparatory to divorce.

Naturally Taylor would stay with her father, but what would happen to me was another matter. My only living relative was Kara Trent, and even if I'd wanted to live with her—which of course, I didn't—she was clearly destined to be serving a jail sentence in the near future.

For the time being, I had to remain in the city to give evidence in various trials, but after that?

"If you decide to return to Simplicity," said Uncle Adrian, "you have my complete support. However, Barrett, you will always have a home here, and frankly, I'd prefer you to stay."

Taylor hadn't said anything. "What do you think?" I finally asked her.

"I'd like you to stay, but maybe you'd be happier back at Simplicity."

Her father looked at her with mock astonishment. "The gods be praised! My daughter is actually thinking of someone else first?"

She gave him a cheeky grin. "You should recognize reverse psychology when you see it, Dad."

"I'll go to Simplicity for a while," I said, "just to see what it feels like." I looked over at Taylor. "I'll probably be back. I've found the Chattering World has more to offer than I imagined."

She gave me an absolutely enchanting smile. "For a red-haired farmie," she said, "you're all right!"

If you enjoyed this book, you may also like to read these titles from Annick Press (**www.annickpress.com**):

The Big Book of Pop Culture:
A How-To Guide for Young Artists
by Hal Niedzviecki
illustrated by Marc Ngui

Join indie-guru and founder of *Broken Pencil* magazine, Hal Niedzviecki, on a how-to journey to creating pop culture.

If you've had it with big corporations deciding what you read, hear, and view, now is the time to reclaim your own cultural expression and share it with others. Find out how to use the tools of modern media: print (self-publishing zines, comics, and books), video (making movies and shows), CD (creating original music) and the indie-paradise of the internet (websites, blogs—even developing video games). Quick and easy do-in-a-day project ideas are included to get you started.

Punctuated by inspiring interviews with young creators and zine-style graphics that capture the spirit of the indie movement, *The Big Book of Pop Culture* is an empowering guide to original artistic expression.

Paperback $14.95 | Hardcover $24.95

Made You Look: How Advertising Works and Why You Should Know

by Shari Graydon
illustrated by Warren Clark

Advertising is everywhere today. A typical North American teen views a staggering 40,000 ads every year on TV alone! With such a vast number of commercials out there, who's helping them decode the messages?

In *Made You Look*, media maven Shari Graydon offers an intriguing exploration of advertising's inner workings. From the earliest roots of advertising to the guerrilla marketers of the 21st century, this revealing book explores where ads come from, where they're going, and how they work.

"Young adults, once they start reading, will find themselves sucked in..."—*Booklist*, starred review

"... a thought-provoking resource... The author delivers the information in an understandable, entertaining manner."—*Publishers Weekly*

"MADE YOU LOOK is an empowering self-defence kit. Graydon strikes just the right tone: direct and upbeat... "—*Quill & Quire*

"... thorough in coverage and thought-provoking... alluringly hip."—*School Library Journal*

"Graydon does not condemn advertising, but she does caution the reader to think about the messages and make a deliberate choice."—*VOYA*

Paperback $14.95 U.S./$16.95 Cdn | Hardcover $24.95

Acknowledgments

With gratitude to my wonderful agent, Margaret Connolly; my truly exceptional editor, Roberta Ivers; and my invaluable publisher, Linsay Knight. My warmest thanks also to everyone at Annick Press and to Elizabeth McLean, eagle-eyed copy editor.

About the Author

Claire Carmichael has written for a wide range of ages, but finds the young adult genre particularly rewarding.

She has a deep interest in science and society, and how we, as individuals, face both the delights and the often daunting problems of our time, as well as the new challenges that will arise in the near future.

In her books Claire explores the meaning of personal identity, the impact of technology, and how we deal with the ceaseless rain of information that impinges on us every day.

Claire divides her time between Australia and America.

Go to www.clairecarmichael.com for more information about the author, and links to discussion downloads about the ideas and themes in *Leaving Simplicity*.